T. G. Stevenson

Four Books of Choice Old Scottish Ballads

MDCCCXXIII-MDCCCXLIV

T. G. Stevenson

Four Books of Choice Old Scottish Ballads
MDCCCXXIII-MDCCCXLIV

ISBN/EAN: 9783744786140

Printed in Europe, USA, Canada, Australia, Japan

Cover: Foto ©Andreas Hilbeck / pixelio.de

More available books at **www.hansebooks.com**

INTERESTING COLLECTIONS

OF

Ballad Poetry, etc.

PUBLISHED OR SOLD BY

THOMAS GEORGE STEVENSON,

Antiquarian and Historical Bookseller,

22 FREDERICK STREET, EDINBURGH.

(At the Sign of Sir Walter Scott's Head.)

" Whose Shop is well known, or ought to be so, by all the true lovers
of curious little old smoke=dried volumes."

Chambers's Illustrations of the Author of Waverley.

Ayrshire Ballads and Songs. Illustrated with Sketches,
Historical, Traditional, Narrative, and Biographical, by
JAMES PATERSON, with Remarks by Captain GRAY. 8vo,
sewed. 4s. 1846–47

" This Selection is curious and good, and no lover of Scottish
Songs ought to be without a copy. The illustrative Notes
and Sketches are highly interesting, and serve to throw
considerable light on the ballad lore of the West."

Ballad-Books: Four Books of Choice Old Scotish Ballads, viz.:—I. A Ballad-Book.—II. A North Countrie Garland.—III. The Ballad-Book; and, IV. A New Book of Old Ballads. Edited originally by Charles Kirkpatrick Sharpe, James Maidment, and George Ritchie Kinloch. *Now First Collected.* Sm. 8vo, *woodcut portraits of the Celebrated Antiquary,* Charles Kirkpatrick Sharpe, *and* Charles Leslie, *alias "Mussel Mou'd Charlie, the Celebrated Ballad-Singer in Aberdeen," &c. Boards.* 26s.   1868

   ⁎ "Only One Hundred and Fifty-Five Copies of this very Remarkable Collection Printed."

Black-Letter Ballads and Broadsides: A Collection of Seventy-Nine, printed during the Reign of Queen Elizabeth, between the years 1559 and 1597. Edited with an Introduction and Illustrative Notes by Halliwell. Sm. 8vo, *boards.* 12s.   1867

   "All of the highest interest and curiosity, presumed to be unique, and hitherto unknown."

Buchanan (George.) Epithalamium on the Marriage of Francis and Mary Queen of Scots. Translated from the Original. 8vo, *stitched.* 2s.   1845

   ⁎ Impression limited to sixty-five copies.

Child's Collection of English and Scottish Ballads. With a Preface, Notes and List of the Principal Collections of Ballads and Songs. 8 vols. 12mo, *boards.* 30s.   1861

Dalyell's (Sir John Graham) Musical Memoirs of Scotland. With Historical Annotations and Notes, illustrative of the Manners and Customs of Scotland, &c. 4to, *embellished with 45 plates, boards.* 42s.   1849

   "This singularly curious and highly interesting work treats chiefly of those Instruments which are recognized in Scotland, with Dissertations on the ' Bagpipe,' Ecclesiastical Ornaments, Modern Performance, the Organ, Wind Instruments, Springs, Bells, Stringed Instruments, Guitar, Lute, Harp, Instruments with Keys, &c."

   "Mr. Laing, in his "*Introduction* to Stenhouse's Illustrations of the Lyric Poetry and Music of Scotland," remarks that ' The Title of this Volume furnishes no very distinct notion of its Contents, which exhibit the result of a long-continued and laborious investigation into the History or Music in Scotland, selected from copious collections on the subject of Scottish History, the accumulations of many years, and accompanied with plates of the various Musical Instruments in use from the earliest dates.' "

₊ ONLY TWO HUNDRED AND FIFTY COPIES PRINTED.

Hamilton (William, of Bangour) Poems and Songs of, Collated with the MSS., and containing several pieces *hitherto unpublished ;* including the Original Prefaces by Dr. ADAM SMITH and LORD ESKGROVE ; with an Introductory Notice, Illustrative Notes, and an Account of the Life of the Author, by JAMES PATERSON. 12mo, *portraits, boards.* 5s.   1850

——————————————————————— THE SAME

ON FINE THICK WRITING PAPER. Sm. 8vo, *portraits by Strange, &c., half-bound morocco, gilt top.* 10s. 6d. 1850

  " He may be reckoned among the earliest of the Scotch Poets who wrote English verse with propriety and taste. We think, therefore, that Mr. Paterson has done good service in producing a new edition of a Scottish Poet, who can still please or interest his countrymen. No pains have been spared to perfect the work. Mr. David Laing has contributed to its pages from his manuscript collections: and Mr. Charles Kirkpatrick Sharpe has drawn upon his memory to enrich its notes and illustrations."

  " The poems of the elegant and amiable Hamilton of Bangour, display regular design, just sentiments, fanciful invention, pleasing sensibility, elegant diction, and smooth versification. The truly beautiful ballad of the ' Braes of Yarrow,' has been almost universally acknowledged to be one of the finest ever written, and would alone have immortalised his name."

Kelly (Thomas, Sixth Earl of) : Minuets, Songs, &c., composed by,—*now for the first time published*, with an Introductory Notice, by C. K. SHARPE. 4to, *portrait and plate, boards.* 10s. 6d.   1839

  " The compositions of this very eminent musical genius were celebrated by his contemporaries, and ought still to be esteemed as an honour to Scotland. He was one of the finest Musical Composers of the age."

₊ ONLY SIXTY COPIES PRINTED.

Kinloch's Ancient Scottish Ballads. Recovered from Tradition, and *never before published ;* with Notes, Historical and Explanatory, and an Appendix containing the *Airs of several of the Ballads.* Sm. 8vo, *boards.* 7s. 6d.   1827

> " The Editor of this Collection has judiciously abstained from all conjectural emendations, and presented to the public, in the shape he received them, a considerable number of Traditionary Ballads, principally obtained from recitation in the Northern Shires."—WILLIAM MOTHERWELL.

> " Various valuable Collections of Ancient Ballad Poetry have appeared of late years, some of which are illustrated with learning and acuteness:—those of Mr. Motherwell and of Mr. Kinloch intimate much taste and feeling for this species of literature."—SIR WALTER SCOTT.

Legendary Ballads of England and Scotland. Edited,
with Notes, by ROBERTS. Sm. 8vo, *portrait and plates, half-bound morocco, gilt top.* 7s. 6d.   1868

> " The bulk of our early Ballads must claim a more than passing attention as long as our language and literature endure."

Lithgow (William, the Celebrated Scotish Traveller):
POETICAL REMAINS, 1618–1660 —I. The Pilgrimes Farewell, to his Natiue Countrey of Scotland, 1618.—II. Scotland's Teares in his Countreyes behalf, 1625.—III. Scotland's Welcome to her Native Sonne, and Soveraigne Lord, King Charles, 1633.—IV. The Gushing Teares of Godly Sorrow, 1640.—V. A Briefe and Summarie Discourse upon that lamentable and dreadfull disaster at Dunglasse, 1640.—VI. Scotland's Parænesis to her dread Soveraign King Charles the Second, 1660. Now FIRST COLLECTED, and Edited, with Bibliographical Notices by JAMES MAIDMENT. Sm. 4to, *boards.* 26s.   1863

*** THIS COLLECTION OF EXCEEDINGLY RARE AND INTERESTING POEMS WAS PRINTED CHIEFLY FOR SUBSCRIBERS, AND THE IMPRESSION WAS LIMITED TO ONE HUNDRED COPIES.

Maidment's Scotish Ballads and Songs. With an Introductory Notice and Illustrative Notes. 12mo, *boards.* 10s. 6d.   1859

> " This interesting collection consists of curious, old, rare, unique Ballads and Songs, which are not to be found in any other collection, with a few from MSS., NOW FOR THE FIRST TIME PRINTED.—The Introductory Notes afford much valuable information."

Mallet's (David) Ballads and Songs. *New Edition*, with Notes and Illustrations, and a Memoir of the Author, by Dr. DINSDALE. Sm. 8vo, *fine plates and facsimiles, boards.* 10s. 6d.   1857

> " These ballads are well known and well loved enough to give an interest to all information respecting either them or their author; and we therefore give our thanks to Mr. Dinsdale for his very diligent work."—*Gentleman's Magazine.*

> " This work bears upon every page evidence that its preparation has been a labour of love. The facts of the poet's life have been collected with great industry, and are narrated with a brevity which contrasts strongly with the abundance of reference to authorities. . . . The poems are annotated with the same care and profusion."—*Notes and Queries.*

Motherwell's (William) Minstrelsy : ANCIENT AND MODERN. A Collection of Scotish Ballads, with an elaborate Historical Introduction and Notes. Sm. 4to, *etchings and plates of music, half-bound morocco, gilt top.* 30s. 1827

> " One of the most interesting and best selected collections ever printed."

Percy's (Bishop) Folio Ballad Manuscript: BALLADS AND ROMANCES, with LOOSE AND HUMEROUS SONGS. Edited, with Illustrative Notes and Introduction, by HALES and FURNIVALL, assisted by CHILD and CHAPPELL. 4 vols. 8vo, *half-bound, uncut.* 42s.   1867–68

> " The reader is here presented with Select Remains of our ancient English Bards and Minstrels, printed from the rare original, FOR THE FIRST TIME IN A COMPLETE UNMUTILATED FORM. As a mere piece of printing—a mass of paper and type—the PERCY BALLADS are wonderfully cheap, and the work is certain to become scarce before long."

Blackley's Review of Bishop Percy's Folio Ballad Manuscript. 8vo, *stitched.* 1s.   1867

Political Ballads of the Seventeenth and Eighteenth Centuries. Annotated by WILKINS. 2 vols. sm. 8vo, *boards.* 10s. 6d.   1860

> " The amusing and often very witty Ballads, commence with the reign of Charles I., and end with that of George II."

Four Books

of Choice Old

Scotish Ballads.

" To many it may appear a foolish labour, this of gathering Old Ballads. Were it worth while, it were easy to vindicate such pursuits, and
to point out their utility ; but as this exception can only be taken by the
superficial thinker and the sciolist, it is of little moment to enlighten
their understanding on the subject. The ignorant are happy, it is said,
and sorry should we be with any impertinent knowledge to disturb their
bliss."   MOTHERWELL.

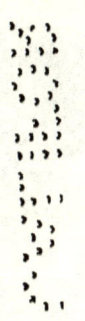

Chas. Kirkpatrick Sharpe

Four Books

of Choice Old

Scotish Ballads,

M.DCCC.XXIII.—M.DCCC.XLIV.

Edinburgh:
Reprinted for Private Circulation.
M.DCCC.LXVIII.

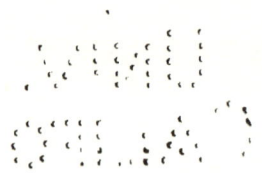

R. Syme & Son, Printers, Edinburgh.

TO

Joseph Walter King Eyton, Esq.,

F. S. A. LOND. AND SCOT.,

THIS

Collection of Reprints,

IS INSCRIBED,

IN TESTIMONY OF RESPECT AND ESTEEM,

BY

HIS MUCH OBLIGED SERVANT,

The Editor.

Preface.

———

THE SERIES OF BALLAD-BOOKS contained in this Collection was originally issued at PRIVATE EXPENSE, chiefly for presentation to the particular friends of their respective Editors.

The IMPRESSIONS printed were exceedingly limited in number, and, consequently, soon became very scarce. Now they are in the language of Bibliopoles, " EXCESSIVELY RARE." Their value, both in a literary and financial point of view, was known to be great; and when by chance any of them was exposed for sale on the dispersion of some eminent collector's library, the competitors were many, and the prices realized extravagant in almost every case.

The recent Publications by the "PERCY," the "WARTON" and the "EARLY ENGLISH TEXT SOCIETIES" having extended the taste for Ballad Lore, and the demand for such works, (many of which are now difficult to procure,) having consequently increased, I have been induced to reprint *literatim*, and to issue in a Collected form, the following "PEARLS OF GREAT PRICE," viz. :—

I.—A Ballad Book. [Edited by CHARLES KIRKPATRICK SHARPE, Edinburgh, 1823.]

The IMPRESSION of this Volume was limited to " THIRTY COPIES."—WILLIAM MOTHERWELL, in the highly valuable and elaborate Historical Introduction prefixed to his " Minstrelsy : Ancient and Modern, Sm. 4to, Glasgow, 1827," remarks that, "'A BALLAD BOOK,' a little fairy volume, under this title, was printed for *private* distribution by its Editor, C. K. Sharpe, Esq. in 1824 [1823]. It contains many curious pieces, ' gathered,' as its address to the ' Courteous Reader' declareth, ' from the mouths of nurses, wet and dry, singing to their babes and sucklings, dairy maids pursuing their vocation in the cow-house, and tenants' daughters while giving the lady (as every Laird's wife was once called,) a spinning day, whilom an anniversary tribute in Annandale.' Besides giving different versions of a number of Ballads, noticed in their proper place, it presents us with the following for the first time, published in a collected shape :—' DYSMAL,' ' GLASGOW PEGGY,' ' FAIR MARGARET OF CRAIGNARGAT,' ' O ERROL IT'S A BONNY PLACE,' and ' RICHIE STORIE.'"

II. — A North Countrie Garland, Edinburgh, M.DCCC.XXIV. [Edited by JAMES MAIDMENT.]

The IMPRESSION of this Volume was limited to "THIRTY COPIES."—Of this Collection MOTHERWELL observes that " A yet more slender volume appeared in the same year, Edited by James Maidment, Esq., and, like the ' Ballad Book,' its impression was limited to thirty copies. Its title is, '*A North Countrie Garland.*' Many of the pieces in it had never before been published. Small as is the volume, it makes considerable addition to our catalogue of Ancient Ballads :—' LORD THOMAS STEWART,' 'THE BURNING OF FRENDREUGH,' ' LORD SALTON AND AUCHANACHIE,' ' BONNY JOHN SETON,' ' BURD ELLEN AND YOUNG TAMLENE,' and ' EPPIE MORRIE.' "

III.—The Ballad Book, Edinburgh, M.DCCC.XXVII. [Edited by GEORGE RITCHIE KINLOCH.]

The IMPRESSION of this Volume was limited to " FORTY COPIES."—" The Ballads in this collection are given as they were taken down from recitation ; and though, no doubt, in many respects requiring emendation, to render them in some instances more intelligible, the Editor has scrupulously abstained from taking any liberties with the text."—The ' BIOGRAPHIA LESLYANA ' is highly interesting.

IV. — A New Book of Old Ballads, Edinburgh, M.DCCC.XLIV. [Edited by JAMES MAIDMENT.]

The IMPRESSION of this Volume was limited to " SIXTY COPIES."—" The chief attraction of this collection consists in the recovery of early versions of two or three popular Scottish Ballads, discovered in a Manuscript Volume in the handwriting of WILLIAM HAMILTON, *younger of Airdrie*, with a few fragments taken down from recitation and from scarce Broadsides."

2

The ILLUSTRATIONS *new* to this COLLECTION OF REPRINTS consist of :—

I.—The PORTRAIT of the " *Celebrated Antiquary*" CHARLES KIRKPATRICK SHARPE, Esq., " *The Scotish Walpole*," Editor not only of " A Ballad Book," but of numerous other highly valuable and interesting works illustrative of Scotish history and poetry, taken from a calotype by Mr. D. O. HILL, the original of which is in my possession.

II. — An interesting full-length PORTRAIT of "CHARLIE LESLIE *of Aberdeenshire*," alias " *Mussel mou'd Charlie, the celebrated Ballad-Singer in Aberdeen*;" copied from an impression of an old copperplate which at one time was the property of the late Mr. PETER BUCHAN, the industrious and successful collector of local and traditionary song, and Editor of " Ancient Ballads and Songs of the North of Scotland, Edinburgh, 1828." The history of this plate I have never been able to ascertain, except that it appeared as a FRONTISPIECE to a small publication by Mr. BUCHAN, entitled, " The Wanderings of Prince Charles and Flora Macdonald, Edinburgh, 1838."

The BIBLIOMANIAC will have infinite pleasure in learning that there is no probability of this collected series ever coming into general circulation, as the impression is strictly limited to ONE HUNDRED AND FIFTY-FIVE COPIES, the greater portion of which being destined for the Cabinets of the Curious, the Reprint, in a few years, will be as difficult to procure as the originals.

T. G. S.

EDINBURGH, 1868.

L' Envoy.

"Therefore begone, my book, stretch forth thy wings, and fly
Amongst the nobles and gentility:
Thou'rt not to sell to scabingers and clowns,
But given to worthy persons of renown.
The number's few I've printed in regard
My charges have been great, and I hope reward;
I caus'd not print many above seven score,
And the printers are engag'd that they shall print no more."

Scot's True History of the name of Scot, 1688.

Contents.

I.—A Ballad Book, 1823.

II.—A North Countrie Garland, 1824.

𝕴𝕴𝕴.—𝕿𝖍𝖊 𝕭𝖆𝖑𝖑𝖆𝖉 𝕭𝖔𝖔𝖐, 1827.

IV.—A New Book of Old Ballads, 1844.

A

Ballad Book.

"She thrusts her right hand into the very bottom of his pannier.—I have nothing, good Lady, but empty bottles! says the ass."

SLAWKENBERGIUS.

TO

Sir Walter Scott, Bart.

THIS TRIFLE,

WHICH THE EDITOR DEEMS MOST

UNWORTHY OF HIS ACCEPTANCE,

IS,

BY HIS KIND PERMISSION,

GRATEFULLY DEDICATED.

Courteous Reader,

As this Book, of which only thirty copies
are printed, shall cost thee nothing, save
a little time thrown away on its perusal,
which most Antiquaries can very well
spare, I will make no apology to thee for
the compiling of it. The truth is, I was
anxious, after this fashion, to preserve a
few Songs that afforded me much delight
in my early youth, and are not to be found
at all, or complete, or in the same shape

in other Collectious. These have been mostly gathered from the mouths of nurses, wet and dry, singing to their babes and sucklings, dairy-maids pursuing their vocation in the cow-house, and tenants' daughters, while giving the Lady (as every Laird's wife was once called,) a spinning day, whilom an anniversary tribute in Annandale. Several, too, were picked up from tailors, who were wont to reside in my father's castle, while misshaping clothes for the children and servants. Though I am sensible that none of these Ballads are of much merit, I regret that my memory doth not now serve me as to many more, the outlines of which alone I remember. Some, indeed, I have suppressed on account of their grossness; confessing, at the same time, that several here printed, are not over delicate; but little will be found to corrupt the imagination, and nothing to inflame the passions.—Sufficit!—I have inserted a few from MS. Collections in my possession, and perhaps shall be tempted by and by, to add a second volume from the same sources.—In the meantime, gentle reader,

HAIL! AND FAREWELL!

I.

Fair Janet.

This Ballad, the subject of which appears to have been very Popular, is Printed as it was Sung by an Old Woman in Perthshire.—The Air is extremely beautiful.

I.

" Ye maun gang to your Father, Janet,
  " Ye maun gang to him soon;
" Ye maun gang to your Father, Janet,
  " In case that his days are dune!"

II.

Janet's awa' to her Father,
  As fast as she could hie;
" O, what's your will wi' me, Father?
  " O, what's your will wi' me?"

III.

" My will wi' you, Fair Janet," he said,
  " It is both bed and board ;
" Some say that ye lo'e sweet Willie,
  " But ye maun wed a French Lord."

IV.

" A French Lord maun I wed, Father ?
  " A French Lord maun I wed ?
" Then by my sooth," quo fair Janet,
  " He's ne'er enter my bed."

V.

Janet's awa' to her chamber,
  As fast as she could go ;
Wha's the first ane that tapped there,
  But sweet Willie, her jo ?

VI.

" O we maun part this love, Willie,
  " That has been lang between ;
" There's a French Lord coming o'er the sea,
  " To wed me wi' a ring ;
" There's a French Lord coming o'er the sea,
  " To wed and tak' me hame."

VII.

" If we maun part this love, Janet,
  " It causeth mickle woe ;
" If we maun part this love, Janet,
  " It makes me into mourning go."

VIII.

" But ye maun gang to your three sisters,
  " Meg, Marion, and Jean ;
" Tell them to come to Fair Janet,
  " In case that her days are dune."

IX.

Willie's awa' to his three sisters,
  Meg, Marion, and Jean ;
" O, haste and gang to Fair Janet,
  " I fear that her days are dune."

·X.

Some drew to them their silken hose,
  Some drew to them their shoon,
Some drew to them their silk manteils,
  Their coverings to put on ;
And they're awa' to Fair Janet,
  By the hie light o' the moon.

* * * * * * *

* * * * * * *

XI.

" O, I have born this Babe, Willie,
 " Wi' mickle toil and pain ;
" Take hame, take hame, your Babe, Willie,
 " For nurse I dare be nane."

XII.

He's tane his young son in his arms,
 And kiss't him cheek and chin—
And he's awa' to his mother's bower,
 By the hie light o' the moon.

XIII.

" O, open, open, mother," he says,
 " O, open, and let me in ;
" The rain rains on my yellow hair,
 " And the dew drops o'er my chin—
" And I hae my young son in my arms,
 " I fear that his days are dune."

XIV.

With her fingers lang and sma',
  She lifted up the pin;
And with her arms lang and sma'.
  Received the baby in.

XV.

" Gae back, gae back, now sweet Willie,
  " And comfort your fair lady;
" For where ye had but ae nourice,
  " Your young Son shall hae three."

XVI.

Willie he was scarce awa',
  And the Lady put to bed,
Whan in and came her Father dear,
  " Make haste, and busk the Bride."

XVII.

" There's a sair pain in my head, Father,
  " There's a sair pain in my side,
" And ill, O ill, am I, Father,
  " This day for to be a Bride."

XVIII.

" O, ye maun busk this bonny bride,
  " And put a gay mantle on ;
" For she shall wed this auld French Lord,
  " Gin she should die the morn."

XIX.

Some pat on the gay green robes.
  And some pat on the brown,
But Janet put on the scarlet robes,
  To shine foremost throw the town.

XX.

And some they mounted the black steed,
  And some mounted the brown,
But Janet mounted the milk-white steed,
  To ride foremost throw the town.

XXI.

" O, wha will guide your horse, Janet ?
  " O, wha will guide him best ?"
" O, wha but Willie, my true love,
  " He kens I lo'e him best !"

XXII.

And whan they came to Marie's kirk,
  To tye the haly ban ;
Fair Janet's cheek looked pale and wan,
  And her colour gaed an cam.

XXIII.

When dinner it was past and done,
  And dancing to begin ;
" O, we'll go take the Bride's maidens,
  " And we'll go fill the ring."

XXIV.

O, ben than came the auld French Lord,
  Saying, " Bride will ye dance wi' me ?"
" Awa', awa', ye auld French Lord,
  " Your face I downa see."

XXV.

O, ben than cam' now sweet Willie,
  He cam' with ane advance ;
" O, I'll go tak' the Bride's maidens,
  " And we'll go tak' a dance."

XXVI.

" I've seen ither days wi' you, Willie,
  " And so has mony mae ;
" Ye would hae danced wi' me mysel',
  Let a' my maidens gae."

XXVII.

O, ben then cam' now sweet Willie,
  Saying, " Bride will ye dance wi' me ?"
" Aye, by my sooth, and that I will,
  " Gin my back should break in three."

XXVIII.

She had nae turned her throw the dance,
  Throw the dance but thrice,
Whan she fell doun at Willie's feet,
  And up did never rise !

XXIX.

Willie's taen the key of his coffer, ·
  And gi'en it to his man,
" Gae hame, and tell my Mother dear,
  " My horse he has me slain ;
" Bid her be kind to my young Son,
  " For Father he has nane."

XXX.

The tane was buried in Marie's kirk,
 And the tither in Marie's quier ;
Out of the tane there grew a birk,
 And the tither a bonny brier.

II.

The two following Songs were remembered
 thirty years ago, by an Old Gentlewoman.—
 The first seems to be a Satire on the Court
 Ladies of Edinburgh.

I.

The lasses o' the Cannogate,
 O, they are wond'rous nice,—
They winna gie a single kiss,
 But for a double price.

B

II.

Gar hang them, gar hang them,
    Heich upon a tree,
For we'll get better up the gate,
    For a bawbee.

III.

As Illustrations of the following Song, vide Sir
    Richard Maitland's Poem beginning,

   " Some wyfis of the Burroustoun,
   " Sa wonder vane ar, and wantoun,
   " In warld they wait not quhat to weir;"

And Sir David Lindsay's supplication against
    Syde Taillis and Mussalit Faces.

---

aw. the Walkin o' the fauld.

I.

I'll gar our gudeman trow
    That I'll sell the ladle,
If he winna buy to me,
    A new side saddle,—

To ride to the kirk, and frae the kirk,
    And round about the toun,—
Stand about, ye fisher jads,
    And gie my goun room !

II.

I'll gar our gudeman trow
    That I'll tak' the fling strings,
If he winna buy to me
    Twelve bonnie goud rings,—
Ane for ilka finger,
    And twa for ilka thoom,—
Stand about, ye fisher jads,
    And gie my goun room !

III.

I'll gar our gudeman trow
    That I'll tak' the glengore,
If he winna fee to me
    Three valets, or four,
To beir my tail up frae the dirt,
    And ush me throw the toun,—
Stand about, ye fisher jads,
    And gie my goun room !

IV.

This stupid Ballad, Printed as it was Sung in
   Annandale, is founded on the well known Story
   of the Prince of Solerno's Daughter; but with
   what uncouth change! Dysmal for Ghismonda
   and Guiscardo transformed into a greasy kitchen
   boy.

   " An ounce of civet, good apothecary,
   " To sweeten my imagination."

The reader will immediately remember Hogarth's
   Picture and Churchill's exclamation—

   " Poor Sigismunda, what a fate was thine."

I.

There was a king, and a glorious king,
   And a king of mickle fame;
And he had daughters only one,
   Lady Dysmal was her name.

II.

He had a boy, and a kitchen boy,
    A boy of mickle scorn;
And she lov'd him lang, and she lov'd him aye,
    Till the grass o'ergrew the corn.

III.

When twenty weeks were gone and past,
    O, she began to greet;
Her petticoats grew short before,
    And her stays they wadna meet.

IV.

It fell upon a winter's night,
    The king could get nae rest;
He cam unto his Daughter dear,
    Just like a wand'ring ghaist.

V.

He cam into her bed chalmer,
    And drew the curtains round,—
" What aileth thee, my Daughter dear,
    " I fear you've gotten wrong?"

VI.

" O, if I have, despise me not,
 " For he is all my joy;
" I will forsake baith Dukes and Earls,
 " And marry your kitchen boy."

VII.

" Go call to me, my merry men all,
 " By thirty and by three;
" Go call to me my kitchen boy,
 " We'll murder him secretlie."

VIII.

There was nae din that could be heard,
 And ne'er a word was said,
Till they got him baith fast and sure,
 Between twa feather beds.

IX.

" Go, cut the heart out of his breast,
 " And put it in a cup of gold;
" And present it to his Dysmal dear,
 " For she is baith stout and bold."

X.

They've cut the heart out of his breast,
    And put it in a cup of gold;
And presented it to his Dysmal dear,
    Who was baith stout and bold.

XI.

" O, come to me, my hinney, my heart,
    " O, come to me, my joy;
" O, come to me, my hinney, my heart,
    " My Father's kitchen boy."

XII.

She's ta'en the cup out of their hands,
    And set it at her bed head;
She wash'd it wi' the tears that fell from her eyes,
    And next morning she was dead.

XIII.

" O, where were ye, my merry men all,
    " Whom I paid meat and wage,
" Ye didna hold my cruel hand,
    " Whan I was in my rage ?"

XIV.

" For gone is a' my heart's delight,
  " And gone is a' my joy;
" For my dear Dysmal she is dead,
  " And so is my kitchen boy."

V.

This Song, from some original words of the Air,
to which Auld Robin Gray was latterly adapted,
appears to have been composed on a similar
melancholy event.

" The bridegroom grat whan the sun gaed down,
" The bridegroom grat whan the sun gaed down,
" And, ' Och,' quo' he, ' It's come o'er soon,'
" The bridegroom grat," &c.

air 'Bootaram Alim'

I.

There lived a man into the west,
  And O! but he was cruel;
Upon his waddin' nicht at e'en,
  He sat up, and grat for gruel.

II.

They brought to him a good sheep's head,
    A napkin, and a towel,—
" Gae tak' your whim-whams a' frae me,
    " And bring me fast my gruel."

III.

The Bride speaks.

" There is nae meal into the hous,
    " What shall I do, my jewel ?"—
" Gae to the pock, and shake a lock,
    " For I canna want my gruel."

IV.

" There is nae milk into the hous,
    " What shall I do, my jewel ?"—
" Gae to the midden, and milk the soo,
    " For I wunna want my gruel."

VI.

Marie Hamilton.

In the Border Minstrelsy is a much more refined edition of this Ballad, which is supposed to relate the misadventure of one of Queen Marie's ladies. It is singular that during the reign of the Czar Peter, one of his Empress's attendants, a Miss Hamilton, was executed for the murder of a natural child,—not her first crime in that way, as was suspected ; and the Emperor, whose admiration of her beauty did not preserve her life, stood upon the scaffold till her head was struck off, which he lifted by the ear, and kissed on the lips. I cannot help thinking, that the two Stories have been confused in the Ballad, for if Marie Hamilton was executed in Scotland, it is not likely that her relations resided beyond seas ; and we have no proof that Hamilton was really the name of the woman who made a slip with the Queen's apothecary.

I.

Word's gane to the kitchen,
    And word's gane to the ha',
That Marie Hamilton gangs wi' bairn.
    To the hichest Stewart of a'.

II.

He's courted her in the kitchen.
    He's courted her in the ha',
He's courted her in the laigh cellar,
    And that was warst of a' !

III.

She's tyed it in her apron,
    And she's thrown it in the sea,
Says, " Sink ye, swim ye, bonny wee babe,
    " You'l ne'er get mair o' me."

IV.

Down then cam the auld Queen,
    Goud tassels tying her hair—
" O, Marie, where's the bonny wee babe,
    " That I heard greet sae sair ?"

V.

" There was never a babe intill my room,
  " As little designs to be ;
" It was but a touch o' my sair side,
  " Come o'er my fair bodie."

VI.

" O, Marie, put on your robes o' black,
  " Or else your robes o' brown,
" For ye maun gang wi' me the night,
  " To see fair Edinbro' town."

VII.

" I winna put on my robes o' black,
  " Nor yet my robes o' brown,
" But I'll put on my robes o' white,
  " To shine through Edinbro' town."

VIII.

When she gaed up the Cannogate,
  She laugh'd loud laughters three ;
But whan she cam down the Cannogate,
  The tear blinded her e'e.

IX.

When she gaed up the Parliament stair,
 The heel cam aff her shee,
And lang or she cam down again,
 She was condemn'd to dee.

X.

When she cam down the Cannogate,
 The Cannogate sae free,
Mony a ladie look'd o'er her window,
 Weeping for this ladie.

XI.

" Ye need nae weep for me," she says,
 " Ye need nae weep for me,
" For had I not slain mine own sweet babe,
 " This death I wadna dee.

XII.

" Bring me a bottle of wine," she says,
 " The best that e'er ye hae,
" That I may drink to my weil wishers,
 " And they may drink to me.

XIII.

" Here's a health to the jolly sailors,
" That sail upon the main,
" Let them never let on to my father and mother,
" But what I'm coming hame.

XIV.

" Here's a health to the jolly sailors,
" That sail upon the sea ;
" Let them never let on to my father and mother,
" That I am here to dee.

XV.

" Oh, little did my mother think,
" The day she cradled me,
" What lands I was to travel through,
" What death I was to dee.

XVI.

" Oh, little did my father think,
" The day he held up me,
" What lands I was to travel through,
" What death I was to dee.

XVII.

" Last night I wash'd the Queen's feet,
   " And gently laid her down ;
" And a' the thanks I've gotten the nicht,
   " To be hang'd in Edinbro' town.

XVIII.

" Last nicht there was four Maries,
   " The nicht there'l be but three ;
" There was Marie Seton, and Marie Beton,*
   " And Marie Carmichael, and me."

---

* In Balfour House, in Fifeshire, is a full-length
Portrait of Marie Beaton.

VII.

Lady Dundonald.

This strange folly was generally sung by a man, with a woman's cap on his head, a distaff, and a spindle. The dialogue, of which the subjoined is only a Fragment, was chanted in recitative. Can this Song possibly allude to Elizabeth, Daughter and heiress of William Cochrane of Cochrane, who married Alexander, a younger Son of John Blair of Blair? Her Father made a settlement of his estate in her favour 1593. At Gosford, a seat of the Earl of Wemyss, is a full length portrait of a hideous old woman, with her spinning implements, and a starved cat, said to be the Lady Dundonald of the Ballad; but to me it appears to be the figure of a Flemish Peasant.

1.

Weel it becomes the Lady Dundonald,
To sit liltin' at her rock,
And weel it becomes the Laird o' Dundonald,
To wear his hodden gray frock !

CHORUS.

Lilty Eery, Lardy Lardy,
Lilty Eery, Lardy Lam.

II.

Enter MARG'ET.

" My Lady, there is a lass at the door wants
" To be feed."—
". What fee does she want ?"—
" Five punds."—
" Five punds is o'er mony punds, to be
" Drawing out the tail o' a rock."
Lilty Eery, &c.

III.

" Tell her I will gee her
" Four punds, and spin a' the
" Backs mysel."
Lilty Eery, &c.

c

IV.

Enter MARG'ET.

" My Lady, what will I tell you noo,

" Isna our kitchen lass wi' bairn !"—

" Wha may that be till ?

" The Laird, I needna speir."

Lilty Eery, &c.

V.

" He has fifteen at the fire-side else,

" And that will mak sixteen,

" And sae it will een ;

" It was me that made him a Laird ;

" But deel speed sic Lairds !"

Lilty Eery, &c.

VI.

" Hear, Marg'et !"—

" What does my Lady want noo ?"—

" Bring ben the brandy bottle, your waas,

" And tak a dram yoursel',

" And gar me tak twa."

Lilty Eery, &c.

VII.

" I think we may as weel

" Tak our ain geer oursels,

" For it is gaein' whether or no."

Lilty Eery, &c.

VIII.

Enter JOHN.

" My Lady, there is company come."—

" Fashious fock, John ; I want nae company,

" I am spinning at my rock."

Lilty Eery, &c.

IX.

" My Lady, the servants is going to their beds,

" They want the doup of a candle."—

" Tell them to put doups and doups thegither,

" And that will gie them licht."

Lilty Eery, &c.

VIII.

I.

Jenny, scho's ta'en a deep surprise,
    And scho's spew'd a' her crowdie;
Her minnie scho ran to seek her a dram,
    But scho stude mair need o' the howdie.

II.

" O, Sandie, dinna ye mind," quo' scho,
    " Whan ye gart me drink the brandy,
" Whan ye yerkit me ow'r amang the braume,
    " And plaid me Houghmagandy !"

IX.

I.

And sae ye've treated me,
   And sae ye've treated me;
I'll never lo'e anither man,
   Sae weil as I've lo'ed thee.

II.

And sae ye've treated me,
   And sae ye've treated me;
The deil pit on your windin' sheet,
   Three hours before you dee!

X.

The Twa Sisters.

Various sets of this Song have been Printed; it was popular both in England and Scotland.— The Air is beautiful.

Air "Bonnie Susie Cleland"

I.

There liv'd twa sisters in a bower,
   Hey Edinbruch, how Edinbruch.
There liv'd twa sisters in a bower,
   Stirling for aye :
The youngest o' them, *the* she was the flower!
of Bonny Sanct Johnstoune that stands upon Tay.

II.

There cam a squire frae the west,
　　Hey Edinbruch, how Edinbruch.
There cam a squire frae the west,
　　Stirling for aye :
He lo'ed them baith, but the youngest best,
at Bonny Sanct Johnstoune that stands upon Tay.

III.

He gied the eldest a gay gold ring,
　　Hey Edinbruch, how Edinbruch.
He gied the eldest a gay gold ring,
　　Stirling for aye :
But he lo'ed the youngest aboon a' thing,
in Bonny Sanct Johnstoune that stands upon Tay.

IV.

" Oh, sister, sister, will ye go to the sea ?
　.　" Hey Edinbruch, how Edinbruch.
" Oh, sister, sister, will ye go to the sea ?
　　" Stirling for aye :
" Our father's ships sail bonnilie,
aest " Bonny Sanct Johnstoune that stands upon Tay."

V.

The youngest sat down upon a stane,
  Hey Edinbruch, how Edinbruch.
The youngest sat down upon a stane,
  Stirling for aye:
The eldest shot the youngest in,
  Bonny Sanct Johnstoune that stands upon Tay.

VI.

" Oh, sister, sister, lend me your hand,
  " Hey Edinbruch, how Edinbruch.
" Oh, sister, sister, lend me your hand,
  " Stirling for aye:
" And you shall hae my gouden fan,
  " Bonny Sanct Johnstoune that stands upon Tay."

VII.

" Oh, sister, sister, save my life,
  " Hey Edinbruch, how Edinbruch,
" Oh, sister, sister, save my life,
  " Stirling for aye:
" And ye shall be the squire's wife,
  " Bonny Sanct Johnstoune that stands upon Tay."

VIII.

First she sank, and then she swam,
  Hey Edinbruch, how Edinbruch.
First she sank, and then she swam,
  Stirling for aye :
Untill she cam to Tweed mill dam,
  Bonny Sanct Johnstoune that stands upon Tay,

IX.

The millar's daughter was baking bread,
  Hey Edinbruch, how Edinbruch.
The millar's daughter was baking bread,
  Stirling for aye:
She went for water, as she had need,
  Bonny Sanct Johnstoune that stands upon Tay.

X.

" Oh, father, father, in our mill dam,
  " Hey Edinbruch, how Edinbruch.
" Oh, father, father, in our mill dam,
  " Stirling for aye :
" There's either a lady, or a milk-white swan,
" Bonny Sanct Johnstoune that stands upon Tay."

XI.

They could nae see her fingers small,
   Hey Edinbruch, how Edinbruch,
They could nae see her fingers small,   .
   Stirling for aye :
Wi' diamond rings they were cover'd all,
   Bonny Sanct Johnstoune that stands upon Tay,

XII.

They could nae see her yellow hair,
   Hey Edinbruch, how Edinbruch,
They could nae see her yellow hair,
   Stirling for aye :
Sae mony knots and platts war there,
   Bonny Sanct Johnstoune that stands upon Tay.

XIII.

They could nae see her lilly feet,
   Hey Edinbruch, how Edinbruch.
They could nae see her lilly feet,
   Stirling for aye :
Her gowden fringes war sae deep,
   Bonny Sanct Johnstoune that stands upon Tay.

XIV.

Bye there cam a fiddler fair,
  Hey Edinbruch, how Edinbruch.
Bye there cam a fiddler fair,
  Stirling for aye :
And he's ta'en three taits o' her yellow hair,
  Bonny Sanct Johnstoune that stands upon Tay.

*   *   *   *   *   *   *

XI.

The Fiddler's Benison.

My blessing gae wi' ye, Jock Rob, Jock Rob,
My blessing gae wi' you, Jock Rob ;
For whan ye come here, ye mak us good cheer,
And gar our blythe bottoms play bob !

XII.

The Soutar and the Soo.

It is very strange, as well as amusing, to observe
how much our Antient Poets detested Soutars;
examples are too numerous to be quoted.

The Soutar gied the Soo a kiss—
" Grumph," quo' scho, " It's for my briss."
" And whare gat ye sae sweet a mou ?"
Quo' the Soutar to the Soo.
" Grumph," quo' scho, " And whare gat ye
" A tongue sae sleekie and sae slee ?"

XIII.

Glenlogie.

Four and twenty nobles sits in the king's ha',
Bonnie Glenlogie is the flower among them a' ;

In came Lady Jean skipping on the floor,
And she has chosen Glenlogie 'mong a' that was there.

She turned to his footman, and thus she did say :
" Oh, what is his name, and where does he stay ?"—

" His name is Glenlogie, when he is from home,
" He is of the gay Gordons, his name it is John."

" Glenlogie, Glenlogie, an' you will prove kind,
" My love is laid on you, I am telling my mind."

He turned about lightly, as the Gordons does a',
" I thanky ou, Lady Jean, my loves is promised awa'.'

She called on her maidens her bed for to make,
Her rings and her jewels all from her to take.

In came Jeanie's father, a wae man was he,
Says, " I'll wed you to Drumfendrich, he has mai:
    gold than he."

Her father's own chaplain, being a man of great skill
He wrote him a letter, and indited it well ;

The first lines he looked at, a light laugh laughed he
But ere he read through it, the tears blinded his e'e.

Oh, pale and wan looked she when Glenlogie cam in
But even rosy grew she when Glenlogie sat down.

" Turn round Jeanie Melville, turn round to this side,
" And I'll be the bridegroom, and you'll be the bride.'

Oh, 'twas a merry wedding, and the portion down told
Oh bonnie Jeanie Melville, who was scarce sixteer
    years old.

XIV.

I.

I went to the mill, but the miller was gone,
I sat me down, and cried ochone!
To think on the days that are past and gone,
Of Dickie Macphalion that's slain.
Shoo, shoo, shoolaroo,
To think on the days that are past and gone,
Of Dickie Macphalion that's slain.

II.

I sold my rock, I sold my reel,
And sae hae I my spinning wheel,
And a' to buy a cap of steel
For Dickie Macphalion that's slain !
Shoo, shoo, shoolaroo,
And a' to buy a cap of steel
For Dickie Macphalion that's slain.

XV.

Glasgow Peggie.

Tune 'Haud awa frae me donald."

I.

As I cam in by Glasgow town,
The Highland troops were a' before me ;
And the bonniest lass that e'er I saw,
She lives in Glasgow, they ca' her Peggie.

II.

I wad gie my bonnie black horse,
So wad I my gude grey naigie,
If I were twa hundred miles in the north,
And nane wi' me but my bonnie Peggie !

III.

Up then spak her father dear,
Dear wow ! but he was wond'rous sorrie—
" Weel may ye steal a cow or a yowe,
" But ye dare nae steal my bonnie Peggie."

IV.

Up then spak her mother dear, *mellow*
Dear wow! but she spak wond'rous sorrie—
" Now since I have brought ye up this length,
" Wad ye gang awa' wi' a Highland fellow?"

V.

He set her on his bonnie black horse,
He set himsel' on his gude gray naigie;
And they have ridden o'er hills and dales,
And he's awa' wi' *their* his bonnie Peggie.

VI.

They have ridden o'er hills and dales,
They have ridden o'er mountains many,
Until they cam to a low low glen,
And there he's lain down wi' his bonnie Peggie.

VII.

Up then spak the Earl of Argyle, *Jean Ellie*
Dear wow! but he spak wond'rous sorrie— *was angry than*
" The bonniest lass in a' Scotland,
" Is off and awa' wi' a Highland fellow."

D

VIII.

Their bed was of the bonnie green grass,
Their blankets war o' the hay sae bonnie ;
He folded his philabeg below her head,
And he's lain down wi' his bonnie Peggie.

IX.

Up then spak the bonnie Lowland lass,
And wow ! but she spak wond'rous sorrie—
" I'se warrant my mither wad hae a gay sair heart,
" To see me lien' here wi' you, my Willie."

X.

" In my father's house there's feather beds,
" Feather beds, and blankets mony ;
" They're a' mine, and they'll sune be thine,
" And what needs your mither be sae sorrie
   " Peggie."

XI.

" Dinna you see yon nine score o' kye,
" Feeding on yon hill sae bonnie ?
" They're a' mine, and they'll sune be thine,
" And what needs your mither be sorrie, Peggie."

XII.

" Dinna ye see yon nine score o' sheep,

" Feeding on yon brae sae bonnie ?

" They're a' mine, and they'll sune be thine,

" And what need's your mither be sorrie for ye."

XIII.

" Dinna ye see yon bonnie white house,

" Shining on yon brae sae bonnie ?

" And I am the Earl of the Isle of Skye,

" And surely my Peggie will be ca'd a lady."

XVI.

Tam o' the Lin.

These Stanzas of a well known Song, have not, I
believe, been hitherto Printed.

I.

Tam o' Lin's Daughter scho sat on the stair,
And, "wow," quo scho, "Father, am na I fair?
" There's mony ane wed wi' an unwhiter skin,"
" The deil whorl't aff," quo Tam o' the Lin.

II.

Tam o' Lin's Daughter scho sat on the brig,
And, "wow," quo scho, "father am na I trig?"
The brig it brak, and she tummel'd in—
" Your tocher's paid," quo Tam o' the Lin.

XVII.

May Collin.

This is a much fuller Set of the Ballad than I ever saw Printed. It is probable that Collin, or Colvin, is a corruption of Colvill; and that Carline Sands means Carlinseugh Sands, on the coast of Forfarshire. Sir John's charm resembles that used by Sir John Colquhoun in the year 1633, and the Glamour of Faa the Egyptian— touching whose amorous adventure, and tragical end, I may here mention some lines expressive of the powers of the husband's family, which I found among the Macfarlane MSS.

" 'Twixt Wigton and the town of Air,
" Portpatrick and the cruives of Cree,
" No man needs think for to byde there,
" Unless he court with Kennedie."

I will only add, that May Collin's appropriation
of her lover's steed, though unromantic, may be
justified by the example of the Princess of Ca-
thay herself. Ariosto informs us that Angelica
was never at a loss for a palfrey ; when Orlando
had seized one, from which she fell, she would
steal another.

" Cerchi pur, ch' altro furto le dia aita,
" D'un' altra bestia, come prima ha fatto."

I.

Oh ! heard ye of a bloody knight,
Lived in the south country ?
For he has betrayed eight ladies fair,
And drowned them in the sea.

II.

Then next he went to May Colin,
She was her father's heir ;
The greatest beauty in the land,
I solemnly declare.

III.

" I am a knight of wealth and might,
" Of townlands twenty-three ;
" And you'll be the lady of them all
" If you will go with me."

IV.

" Excuse me, then, Sir John," she says,
" To wed I am too young—
" Without I have my parents' leave,
" With you I darena gang."

V.

" Your parents' leave you soon shall have,
" In that they will agree ;
" For I have made a solemn vow,
" This night you'll go with me."

VI.

From below his arm he pulled a charm,
And stuck it in her sleeve;
And he has made her go with him,
Without her parents' leave.

VII.

Of gold and silver she has got
With her twelve hundred pound;
And the swiftest steed her father had,
She has ta'en to ride upon.

VIII.

So privily they went along,
They made no stop or stay,
Till they came to the fatal place,
That they call Bunion Bay.

IX.

It being in a lonely place,
And no house there was nigh,
The fatal rocks were long and steep,
And none could hear her cry.

X.

" Light down," he said, " Fair May Collin,
" Light down and speak with me,
" For here I've drowned eight ladies fair,
" And the ninth one you shall be."

XI.

" Is this your bowers and lofty towers,
" So beautiful and gay,
" Or is it for my gold," she said,
" You take my life away?"

XII.

" Strip off," he says, " thy jewels fine,
" So costly and so brave,
" For they are too costly and too fine,
" To throw in the sea wave."

XIII.

" Take all I have my life to save,
" Oh, good Sir John, I pray,
" Let it ne'er be said you killed a maid,
" Upon her wedding day."

XIV

" Strip off," he says, " thy Holland smock,
" That's bordered with the lawn,
" For it's too costly and too fine,
" To rot on the sea sand."

XV.

" Oh, turn about, Sir John," she said,
" Your back about to me,
" For it never was comely for a man
" A naked woman to see."

XVI.

But as he turned him round about,
She threw him in the sea,
Saying, " Lie you there, you false Sir John,
" Where you thought to lay me."

XVII.

" Oh, lie you there, you traitor false,
" Where you thought to lay me,
" For though you stripped me to the skin,
" Your clothes you've got with thee."

XVIII.

Her jewels fine she did put on,
So costly rich and brave,
And then with speed she mounts his steed,
So well she did behave.

XIX.

That lady fair being void of fear,
Her steed being swift and free,
And she has reached her father's gate,
Before the clock struck three.

XX.

Then first she called the stable groom,
He was her waiting man ;
Soon as he heard his lady's voice,
He stood with cap in hand.

XXI.

" Where have you been, Fair May Collin,
" Who owns this dapple grey ?"
" It is a found one," she replied,
" That I got on the way."

XXII.

Then out bespoke the wily parrot,
Unto fair May Collin—
" What have you done with false Sir John,
" That went with you yestreen ?"

XXIII.

" Oh, hold your tongue my pretty parrot,
" And talk no more of me,
" And where you had a meal a day,
" Oh, now you shall have three !"

XXIV.

Then up bespoke her father dear,
From his chamber where he lay—
" What aileth thee, my pretty Poll,
" That you chat so long or day?"

XXV.

" The cat she came to my cage door,
" The thief I could not see,
" And I called to Fair May Collin.
" To take the cat from me."

XXVI.

Then first she told her father dear,
The deed that she had done,
And next she told her mother dear,
Concerning false Sir John.

XXVII.

" If this be true, Fair May Collin,
" That you have told to me,
" Before I either eat or drink,
" This false Sir John I'll see."

XXVIII.

Away they went with one consent,
At dawning of the day ;
Until they came to Carline Sands,
And there his body lay.

XXIX.

His body tall, by that great fall,
By the waves tossed to and fro,
The diamond ring that he had on,
Was broke in pieces two.

XXX.

And they have taken up his corpse,
To yonder pleasant green,
And there they have buried false Sir John,
For fear he should be seen.

XVIII.

Tune—" Birks of Abergeldie."

I.

My mither built a wee wee house,
A wee wee house, a wee wee house,
My mither built a wee wee house,
To keep me frae the men, O!

The wa's fell in, and I fell out,
The wa's fell in, and I fell out,
The wa's fell in, and I fell out,
Amang the merry men, O!

II.

How can I keep my maidenhead,
My maidenhead, my maidenhead,
How can I keep my maidenhead,
Amang sae mony men, O!
Ane auld mouldy maidenhead,
Ane auld mouldy maidenhead,
Ane auld mouldy maidenhead,
Seven years and ten, O!

III.

The captain bad a guinea for 't,
A guinea for 't, a guinea for 't,
The Captain bad a guinea for 't,
The Colonel he bad ten, O!
The Sergeant he bad naething for 't,
Bad naething for 't, bad naething for 't,
The Sergeant he bad naething for 't,
And he cam farrest ben, O!

XIX.

In the month of July 1589, at the Drum, near
Dalkeith, William master of Somerville acciden-
tally killed his brother John, with whom he had
ever lived in the most affectionate manner, by
the unexpected discharge of his pistol.—(Me-
morie of the Sómervilles vol. 1. p. 466.) This
event I am convinced, is the origin of the following Ballad, of which a fuller and more correct
edition is to be found in Jamieson. As to Kirk-
land, my copy has only kirk-yard, till the last
verse, where *Land* has been added from conjec-
ture. Kirkland, or Inchmurry, is in Perthshire.
—N. B. a similar accident happened in the
Stair Family 1682.

I.

There were twa brethren in the north,
They went to the school * thegither ;
The one unto the other said,
Will you try a warsle afore ?"

---

* Chase is sometimes substituted for School.

II.

They warsled up, they warsled down,
Till Sir John fell to the ground,
And there was a knife in Sir Willie's pouch,
Gied him a deadlie wound.

III.

" Oh, brither dear, take me on your back,
" Carry me to yon burn clear,
" And wash the blood from off my wound,
" And it will bleed nae mair."

IV.

He took him up upon his back,
Carried him to yon burn clear,
And wash'd the blood from off his wound,
But aye it bled the mair.

V.

" Oh, brither dear, take me on your back,
" Carry me to yon kirk-yard,
" And dig a grave baith wide and deep,
" And lay my body there."

E

VI.

He's ta'en him up upon his back,
Carried him to yon kirk-yard;
And dug a grave baith deep and wide,
And laid his body there.

VII.

" But what will I say to my father dear,
" Gin he chance to say, Willie whar's John ?"
" Oh, say that he's to England gone,
" To buy him a cask of wine."

VIII.

" And what will I say to my mother dear,
" Gin she chance to say, Willie whar's John ?"
" Oh, say that he's to England gone,
" To buy her a new silk gown."

IX.

" And what will I say to my sister dear,
" Gin she chance to say, Willie whar's John ?"
" Oh, say that he's to England gone,
" To buy her a wedding ring."

X.

" But what will I say to her you lo'e dear,
" Gin she cry, Why tarries my John ?"
" Oh, tell her I lie in Kirk-land fair,
" And home again will never come."

XX.

In the year 1640, Airlie Castle was destroyed by
the Marquis of Argyll,—a nobleman never ac-
cused of Incontinence, as might be supposed from
this Ballad, which is erroneous in another point,
at least—no Lady Ogilvie had eleven Sons—the
first Earl's wife had three, his daughter-in-law,
who is probably the heroine of the Song, only
one—she herself was a daughter of Lord Banff.

I.

It fell on a day, and a bonny simmer day,
  When green grew aits and barley,
That there fell out a great dispute,
  Between Argyll and Airlie.

II.

Argyll has raised an hunder men,
  An hunder harness'd rarely,
And he's awa' by the back of Dunkell,
  To plunder the Castle of Airlie.

III.

Lady Ogilvie looks o'er her bower window,
  And oh, but she looks weary;
And there she spy'd the great Argyll,
  Come to plunder the bonny House of Airlie.

IV.

" Come down, come down, my Lady Ogilvie,
  " Come down, and kiss me fairly."
" O, I winna kiss the fause Argyll,
  " If he should na leave a standing stane in Airlie."

V.

He hath taken her by the left shoulder,
  Says, " Dame, where lies thy dowry?"
" Oh, it's east and west yon wan water side,
  " And it's down by the banks of the Airlie."

VI.

They hae sought it up, they hae sought it down,
　　They hae sought it maist severely ;
Till they fand it in the fair plumb tree,
　　That shines on the bowling green of Airlie.

VII.

He hath taken her by the middle sae small,
　　And, O, but she grat sairly :
And laid her down by the bonny burn-side,
　　Till they plundered the Castle of Airlie.

VIII.

" Gif my gude Lord war here this night,
　　" As he is with King Charlie,
" Neither you nor ony ither Scottish Lord,
　　" Durst awow to the plundering of Airlie.

IX.

" Gif my gude Lord war now at hame,
　　" As he is with his King,
" There durst nae a Campbell in a' Argyll,
　　" Set fit on Airlie green.

X.

" Ten bonny sons I have born unto him,
  " The eleventh ne'er saw his daddy,
" But though I had an hundred mair,
  " I'd gie them a' to King Charlie."

XXI.

Bessy Bell and Mary Gray died of the plague,
   communicated by their Lover, in the year 1645.
   Their romantic history may be found in Pen-
   nant's Tour, and in the Statistical Account of
   Scotland.   The more modern words of this Ballad were composed by Allan Ramsay.

I.

O Bessie Bell and Mary Gray,
   They war twa bonnie lasses !
They bigget a bower on yon burn-brae,
   And theekit it o'er wi' rashes.

They theekit it o'er wi' rashes green,
  They theekit it o'er wi' heather,
But the pest cam frae the burrows town,
  And slew them baith thegither!

II.

They thought to lye in Methven kirk yard,
  Amang their noble kin,
But they maun lye in Stronach Haugh,
  To biek forenent the sin.
And Bessy Bell and Mary Gray,
  They war twa bonnie lasses!
They biggit a bower on yon burn brae,
  And theekit it o'er wi' rashes.

XXII.

O gin ye war dead, Gudeman,
And a green sod on your heid, Gudeman;
Than I wad war my widowhood,
Upon a rantin' Highlandman!
There's a sheep's heid in the pat, Gudeman,
A sheep's heid in the pat, Gudeman,
The broo to me, the horns to thee,
An' the flesh to our John Highlandman.

CHORUS.

Sing, round about the fire wi' a rung scho ran,
An' round about the fire wi' a rung scho ran,
An' round about the fire wi' a rung scho ran,
" Had awa' your blue breeks frae me, Gudeman."

XXIII.

The following Song used to be sung by a gentleman very eminent at the Scottish Bar, who was
born in the year 1680.

TUNE—" Gramachree."

Last night I dreamt my Peggy
  Was in beneath the bed;
And up I got upo' my doup,
  And oh! but I was glad.
I pat my hand beneath the bed
  To tak her be the lug,
But instead o' my dear Peggy,
  I gat the water mug!

XXIV.

This gross old ditty is founded on a Story in Le Moyen de Parvenir, a book of which the extreme wit is at least equalled by its beastliness.

I.

Our gude wife's wi' bairn, and that's of a lad,
And scho's ta'en a greenin' for a fish crab.
　　With my hey jing, &c.

II.

Up gat our gude man, and cleekit to his claithes,
And he's awa' to the sea-side, trippin' on his taes.
　　With my hey, &c.

III.

" Have ye ony crab-fish?—one, two, three."—
" Tippence is the price o' them gin you and I'll agree."
　　With my hey, &c.

IV.

He's pu'd out his purse, and bought the biggest ane,
He's put it in his nicht mutch, and he's come toddlin
hame.

> With my hey, &c.

V.

He wadna pit it on the dresser, for fyling a' the dishes,
But he pat it in the chalmer pat, where our gude wife

> With my hey, &c.

VI.

Up gat the gude wife, an' for to mak her dam,
Up gat the crab-fish, and took her be the wame.

> With my hey, &c.

VII.

Up gat the gude man, to redd the fish's claws,
Up gat the crab-fish, and took him by the nose.

> With my hey, &c.

_____

XXV.

Andrew Car.

CHORUS.
Hey for Andrew, Andrew,
Hey for Andrew Car!
He gaed to bed to the lass,
And forgot to bar the door!

I.

Andrew Car is cunnin',
And Andrew Car is slee,
And Andrew Car is winnin',
And Andrew Car for me
    Sing hey for Andrew, &c.

II.

O it was Andrew Car,
O it was him indeed;
O it was Andrew Car,
Wha gat my maidenhead.
 Sing hey for Andrew, &c.

————

XXVI.

The Haggis o' Dunbar.

Hey, the Haggis o' Dunbar,
 Fatharalinkum Feedle;
Mony better, few waur,
 Fatharalinkum Feedle.

For to mak this Haggis nice,
 Fatharalinkum, &c.
They pat in a peck o' lice,
 Fatharalinkum, &c.

II.

For to mak this Haggis fat,
    Fatharalinkum, &c.
They pat in a scabbit cat,
    Fatharalinkum Feedle.

*   *   *   *   *   *

———

XXVII.

He's a bonny bonny lad that's a courting me,
He's a bonny bonny lad that's a courting me;
He's cripple of a leg, and blind of an e'e,
He's a bonny bonny lad that's a courting me!

*   *   *   *   *   *   *

XXVIII.

Fair Margaret of Craignargat.

Craignargat is a promontory in the Bay of Luce—
though almost surrounded by the Barony of
Mochrum, it was long possessed by a branch of
the family of Macdowall, which was probably
our Heroine's surname.—On the head of Fair
Margaret's lovers, it may be remarked, that the
Agnews of Lochnaw are a very ancient family,
and hereditary sheriffs of Wigton.—The Gordon mentioned, was probably Gordon of Craigh-
law, whose castle was situated about five miles
from Craignargat, in the parish of Kirkcowan,
considered so remote before the formation of
military roads, that the local proverb says,—
" Out of the world, and into Kirkcowan."—
The Hays of Park, dwelt on the coast, about
six miles from Craignargat ; but it is singular,
that the Lady is not complimented with a Dunbar as her lover, the Place of Mochrum, as the
old tower is called, being only two miles from
her reputed residence.

I.

Fair Marg'ret of Craignargat,
 Was the flow'r of all her kin,
And she's fallen in love with a false young man,
 Her ruin to begin.

II.

The more she lov'd, the more it prov'd,
 Her fatal destiny;
And he that sought her overthrow,
 Shar'd of her misery.

III.

Before that lady she was born,
 Her mother, as we find,
She dreamt she had a daughter fair,
 That was both dumb and blind.

IV.

But as she sat in her bow'r door,
 A viewing of her charms,
There came a raven from the south,
 And pluck'd her from her arms.

V.

Three times on end she dreamt this dream,
 Which troubled sore her mind,
That from that very night and hour,
 She could no comfort find.

VI.

Now she has sent for a wise woman,
 Liv'd nigh unto the port,
Who being call'd, instantly came,
 That lady to comfort.

VII.

To her she told her dreary dream,
 With salt tears in her eye,
Hoping that she would read the same,
 Her mind to satisfy.

VIII.

" Set not your heart on children young,
 " Whate'er their fortune be,
" And if I tell what shall befal,
 " Lay not the blame on me.

F

IX.

" The raven which you dreamed of,
  " He is a false young man,
" With subtile heart and flatt'ring tongue,
  " Your daughter to trepan.

X.

" Both night and day, 'tis you I pray,
  " For to be on your guard,
" For many are the subtile wyles,
  " By which youth are ensnar'd."

XI.

When she had read the dreary dream,
  It vex'd her more and more,
For Craignargat of birth and state,
  Liv'd nigh unto the shore.

XII.

But as in age her daughter wax'd,
  Her beauty did excel,
All the ladies far and near,
  That in that land did dwell.

XIII.

The Gordon, Hay, and brave Agnew,
 Three knights of high degree,
Unto the dame a courting came,
 All for her fair beauty.

XIV.

Which of these men they ask'd her then,
 That should her husband be ?
But scornfully she did reply,
 " I'll wed none of the three."

XV.

" Since it is so, where shall we go,
 " A match for thee to find,
" That art so fair and beautiful,
 " That none can suit thy mind ?"

XVI.

With scorn and pride she answer made,
 " You'll ne'er choice one for me,
" Nor will I wed against my mind,
 " For all their high degree."

XVII.

The brave Agnew, whose heart was true,
   A solemn vow did make,
Never to love a woman more,
   All for that lady's sake.

XVIII.

To counsel this lady was deaf,
   To judgement she was blind,
Which griev'd her tender parents dear,
   And troubled sore their mind.

XIX.

From the Isle of Man a courter came,
   And a false young man was he,
With subtile heart and flatt'ring tongue,
   To court this fair lady.

XX.

This young man was a bold outlaw,
   A robber and a thief,
But soon he gain'd this lady's heart,
   Which caused all their grief.

XXI.

" O will you wed," her mother said,
" A man you do not know,
" For to break your parents' heart,
" With shame but and with woe ?"

XXII.

" Yes I will go with him," she said,
" Either by land or sea,
" For he's the man I've pitched on,
" My husband for to be."

XXIII.

" O let her go," her father said,
" For she shall have her will,
" My curse and mallison she's get,
" For to pursue her still."

XXIV.

" Your curse, father, I dont regard,
" Your blessing I'll ne'er crave,
" To the man I love, I'll constant prove,
" And never him deceive."

XXV.

On board with him fair Marg'ret's gone,
  In hopes his bride to be;
But mark you well, and I shall tell,
  Of their sad destiny.

XXVI.

They had not sail'd a league but five,
  Till the storm began to rise;
The swelling seas ran mountains high,
  And dismal were the skies.

XXVII.

In deep despair, that lady fair,
  For help aloud she cries,
While crystal tears, like fountains ran,
  Down from her lovely eyes.

XXVIII.

" O! I have got my father's curse,
  " My pride for to subdue,
" With sorrows great my heart will break,
  " Alas! what shall I do?

XXIX.

" O ! were I at my father's house,
  " His blessing to receive,
" Then on my bended knees I'd fall,
  " His pardon for to crave.

XXX.

" To aid my grief, there's no relief,
  " To speak it is in vain,
" Likewise my loving parents dear,
  " I ne'er shall see again."

XXXI.

The wind and waves did both conspire,
  The lives for to devour,
That gallant ship that night was lost,
  And never was seen more.

XXXII.

When tidings to Craignargat came,
  Of their sad overthrow,
It griev'd her tender parents' heart,
  Afresh began their woe.

XXXIII.

Of the dreary dream that she had seen,
  And often thought upon,—
" O fatal news," her mother cries,
  " My darling she is gone!

XXXIV.

" O fair Marg'ret, I little thought,
  " The seas should be thy grave,
" When first thou left thy father's house,
  " Without thy parents' leave."

XXXV.

May this tragedy a warning be,
  To children while they live,
That they may love their parents dear,
  Their blessing to receive.

XXIX.

𝕶𝖊𝖒𝖕𝖞 𝕶𝖆𝖞𝖊.

This Song my learned readers will perceive to be
of Scandinavian origin ; and that the wooer's
name was probably suggested by Sir Kaye's of
the Round Table, whose Lady failed to prove
her chastity in the troublesome affair of the
Mantle.———The description of Bengoleer's
daughter resembles that of the enchanted damsel who appeared to courteous King Henrie.—
N.B.—This, and the following Ballad, should
have been placed much earlier in the series.

I.

Kempy Kaye's a wooing gane,
  Far far ayont the sea,
An' he has met with an auld auld man,
  His gudefather to be.

II.

" Gae scrape yeersel, and gae scart yeersel,
    " And mak your bruchty face clean,
" For the wooers are to be here the nicht,
    " And yeer body's to be seen.*

III.

" What's the matter wi' you, my fair maiden,
    " You look so pale and wan ?
" I'm sure you was once the fairest maiden,
    " That ever the sun shined on."

IV.

Sae they scrapit her, and they scartit her,
    Like the face of an assy pan ;
And in cam Kempy Kaye himself,
    A clever and tall young man.

Var.—" For Kempy Kaye's to be here the nicht,
    " Or else the morn at een."

V.

His teeth they were like tether sticks,
  His nose was three feet lang;
Between his shouthers was ells three,
  Between his een a span.

VI. .

" I'm coming to court your dochter dear,
  " An' some pairt of your gear."
" An' by my sooth," quo' Bengoleer,
  " She'll sair a man o' weir."

VII.

" My dochter she's a thrifty lass,
  " She span seven year to me,
" An' if it war weil counted up,
  " Full ten wobs it would be."

VIII.

He led his dochter by the han',
  His dochter ben brought he;
" O, is not she the fairest lass,
  " That's in great Christendye ?'

IX.

Ilka hair intil her head,
   Was like a heather cow,
And ilka louse aninder it,
   Was like a lintseed bow. *

X.

She had lauchty teeth, an' kaily lips,
   An' wide lugs fu' o' hair;
Her pouches fu' o' pease meal daigh,
   War hinging down her spare.

XI.

Ilka ee intil her head,
   Was like a rotten ploom,
An' down down browit was the quean,
   An' sairly did she gloom.

XII.

Ilka nail upon her hand,
   Was like an iron rake,

---

   * *Var.*—Was like a brucket yowe.

An' ilka teeth into her head,
  Was like a tether stake.

XIII.

She gied to him a gay gravat,
  O' the auld horse's sheet;
And he gied her a gay gold ring,
  O' the auld couple reet. *

  *   *   *   *   *   *   *

---

* *i. e.* Root.

XXX.

Among the Songs enumerated in the Complainte
of Scotland, (1549) is, " The frog cam to the
myl dur," probably founded on the same legend
with this, which has a chorus, " Cuddie alone
and I," &c. not worthy of insertion.   In November 1580, the Stationers licenced to E. White,
" A ballad of a most strange wedding of the
frogge and the mouse," which has since frequently appeared in a more modern shape.—See
also in D'Urfrey's Pills, vol. 5th, " A ditty on
a high amour at St. James's, the words by Mr
D'Urfrey, and set to a comical tune."

There lived a puddy in a well,
And a merry mouse in a mill.

Puddy he'd a wooin' ride,
Sword and pistol by his side,

Puddy cam to the mouse's wonne,
" Mistress mouse, are you within?"

" Yes, kind Sir, I am within,
" Saftly do I sit and spin."

" Madame, I am come to woo,
" Marriage I must have of you."

" Marriage I will grant you nane,
" Till uncle rotten he comes hame."

" Uncle rotten's now come hame,
" Fye gar busk the bride alang."

Lord rotten sat at the head o' the table,
Because he was baith stout and able.

Wha is't that sits next the wa',
But lady mouse baith jimp and sma'?

Wha is't that sits next the bride,
But the sola puddy wi' his yellow side? *

Var.—Wha sat at the table fit,
      Wha but froggy and his lame fit?

Syne cam the dewk but and the drake,
The dewk took the puddy and gart him squaik.

Than cam in the carle cat,
Wi' a fiddle on his back ;
" Want ye ony music here ?" *

The puddy he swam down the brook,
The drake he catch'd him in his fluke.

The cat he pu'd lord rotten down,
The kittlens they did claw his crown.

But lady mouse baith jimp and sma',
Crept into a hole beneath the wa' ;
" Squeak," quo' she, " I'm weel awa'."

---

* *Var.*—Then in cam the gude grey cat,
  Wi' a' the kittlens at her back.

XXXI.

The following extract from a letter addressed by
   Keith of Benholm to Captain Brown at Paris,
   explains the subject of this Ballad, which was
   preserved by the peasantry of Annandale, probably owing to the circumstances of Lord Southesque, Lady Errol's brother, being at one time
   possessor of Hoddam Castle—" You may have
   heard ere this of Glencairne's marriage with
   the Countess Dowager of Tweddell, mother in
   lawe to your cousin; and what accessione of
   French landes Glencairne's son is lyke to bring
   to his familie, by a cadet of their hous and
   name, a French marquis, who hath carried my
   Lord Kilmaurs, and his brother, to France for
   that effect.—Then the death of your cousin's

G

lady, my Lady Wigtoune ; with that of the
Erll of Annandell, Bauvaird by his death be-
coming Viscount Stormont and Lord Scoon.—
Lastly, the sadd (and not lyke heard of in this
land amongst eminent persons) story of the
Erll of Errol's impotencie, which is lyke, being
cum to publick hearing, to draw deeper betuix
him and Southesk, than is alledgit it hath done
'twixt him and Southesk's daughter. These are
the meane emergents we are taken up with,
whilst beyond sea empyres are overturning."—
Scoone, 22d. Feb. 1659.

I.

O Errol it's a bonny place,
It stands in yonder glen ;
The lady lost the rights of it,
The first night she gaed hame.

CHORUS.

A waly, and a waly,
According as ye ken ;
The thing we ca' the ranting o't,
Our Lady lies her lane, O !

II.

" What need I wash my apron,
" Or hing it on yon door,
" What need I truce my petticoat,
" It hangs even down before !"
A waly, &c.

III.

Errol's up to Edinburgh gaen,
That bonny burrows town !
He has chused the Barber's daughter,
The toss of a' that town.
A waly, &c.

IV.

He's ta'en her by the milk-white hand,
He's led her o'er the green,

And twenty times he kist her,
Before his Lady's een.
    A waly, &c.

V.

" Look up, look up, now Peggy,
" Look up and think nae shame,
" For I'll give thee five hundred pound,
" To buy to thee a gown !"
    A waly, &c.

VI.

" Look up, look up, now Peggy,
" Look up and think nae shame ;
" For I'll gie thee five hundred pound,
" To bear to me a son."
    A waly, &c.

VII.

" Your name is Kate Carnegie,
" And I'm Sir Gilbert Hay ;
" I'll gar your father sell his lands,
" Your tocher gude to pay."
    A waly, &c.

VIII.

" Now he may take her back again,

" Do wi' her what he can,

" For Errol canna please her,

" Nor ane o' a' his men."

    A waly, &c.

IX.

" Go fetch to me a pint of wine,

" Go fill it to the brim ;

" That I may drink my gude Lord's health,

" 'Tho' Errol be his name."

    A waly, &c.

X.

She has taen the glass into her hand,

She has putten poison in ;

She has sign'd it to her dorty lips,

But ne'er a drop went in.

    A waly, &c.

XI.

Up then spak a little Page,

He was o' Errol's kin,

" Now fie upon ye, lady gay,
" There's poison there within."
    A waly, &c.

XII.

" It's hold your hand, now Kate," he says,
" Hold it back again,
" For Errol shall not drink on't,
" Nor none of all his men."
    A waly, &c.

XIII.

She has taen the sheets into her arms,
She has thrown them o'er the wa';
" Since I maun gae maiden hame again,
" Awa' Errol awa'."
    A waly, &c.

XIV.

She's down the back o' the garden,
And O! as she did murne!
" How can a warkman crave his wage,
" When he never wrought a turn?"

A waly, and a waly,
According as ye ken;
The thing we ca' the ranting o't,
Our Lady lies her lane, O !

XXXII.

Richie Storie.

TUNE—" Braw Lads o' Galla Water."

John, third Earl of Wigton, had six Sons, and
three Daughters.—The second, Lady Lillias
Fleming, was so indiscreet as to marry a footman, by whom she had issue.—She and her
husband assigned her provision to Lieutenant-
Colonel John Fleming, who discharged her re-
nunciation, dated in October 1673.

aw "Huntingtower"

I.

The Erle o' Wigton had three daughters,
O braw wallie! but they were bonnie;
The youngest o' them, and the bonniest too,
Has fallen in love wi' Richie Storie.

II.

" Here's a letter for ye, madame,
" Here's a letter for ye, madame,
" The Erle o' Home wad fain presume,
" To be a suitor to ye, madame."

III.

" I'l hae nane o' your letters, Richie,
" I'l hae nane o' your letters, Richie,
" For I've made a vow, and I'l keep it true,
" That I'l have none but you, Richie."

IV.

" O do not say so, madame,
" O do not say so, madame,
" For I have neither land nor rent,
" For to maintain you o', madame."

V.

" Ribands ye maun wear, madame,

" Ribands ye maun wear, madame,

" With the bands about your neck,

" O' the goud that shines sae clear, madame."

VI.

" I'd lie ayont a dyke, Richie,

" I'd lie ayont a dyke, Richie,

" And I'l be aye at your command,

" And bidding whan ye like, Richie."

VII.

O, he's gane on the braid braid road,

And she's gane through the broom sae bonnie,

Her silken robes down to her heels,

And she's awa' wi' Richie Storie.

VIII.

This lady gade up the Parliament stair,

Wi' pendles in her lugs sae bonnie,

Mony a lord lifted his hat,

But little did they ken she was Richie's lady.

IX.

Up then spak the Erle o' Home's lady,
" Was na ye richt sorrie, Annie,
" To leave the lands o' bonnie Cumbernauld,
" And follow Richie Storie, Annie ?"

X.

" O! what need I be sorrie, madame,
" O! what need I be sorrie, madame,
" For I've got them that I like best,
" And war ordained for me, madame !"

XI.

" Cumbernauld is mine, Annie,
" Cumbernauld is mine, Annie,
" And a' that's mine, it shall be thine,
" As we sit at the wine, Annie."

XXXIII.

The following Fragment I cannot illustrate, either from history or tradition.—Sir William Murray, third son of Sir William Murray of Tullibardine, married Margaret Barclay, the heiress of Arngosk and Kippo, in the reign of King James IV.; but it is very unlikely that the Ballad alludes to that match, particularly as it is remembered to have concluded with the Lady's restoration to her friends,—a finale not uncommon in such cases; with which, by the way, our Scottish annals abound.—*Ex. grat.* A. D. 1336. Allan of Winton forcibly carried off the young heiress ef Seton; this produced a feud in Lothian, some favouring the ravisher, while others sought to bring him to punishment. Fordun says, that on this occasion an hundred ploughs

in Lothian were laid aside from labour. Master
Bowy, in his very curious MS. History of the
House of Glenurquhay, informs us, that " John
Mackrom Macalaster M'Gregor, in anno ——,
ravischit Helene Campbell, dochtir to Sir Colene
Campbell of Glenurquhay, knicht. This Helene
Campbell was widow, and Lady of Lochbuy, and
she was ravischit. The foresaid John was not
richteous air to the M'Gregor, but was principal
of the Clan Donlogneir."—Sir Colin, " wha de-
partit this lyfe in the Tour of Straphillane, 24th
Sept. 1480," understanding that his daughter
had become reconciled to her forced marriage,
waylaid his son-in-law at the hill of Drummond,
slew him, and cutting off his head, put it into
a basket, and covered it with apples.—This, as
an acceptable present, he sent to his daughter,
by a messenger, charged not to mention what
was concealed at the bottom.—In the pedigree
of the Clan Gregor, it is said that Malcolm
M'Gregor *married the lady with a view to conci-
liate the differences between the two families,* and

that she composed a mournful song upon his
death, which is still preserved : probably the
very ditty now attributed to Rob Roy's widow.
Bothwell's violence to Queen Marie is well
known. In the year 1591, Lord Fountainhall
notes from the Criminal Records of Edinburgh,
" Dame Jean Ramsay, Lady Warriston, (she
was of the house of Dalheusy), and Advocate,
contra Robert Carncroce, called Meikle Rob,
and others, for ravishing of her in March last,
contrare to the acts of Parliament."—1594, "the
14th of August, Christian Johnstoun, ane widow in Edinburgh, revest be Patrick Aikenhead.
The towne wes put in ane grate fray be the ring-
ing of the common bell ; the said Christiane
wes followit and brocht back fra him, sua that
the said Patrick got no advantage of her."—
Birrell's Diary.—In the year 1680, Patrick
Carnegie, son to the Earl of Northesk, carried
off by force from the house of Pilcoge, Mary
Gray, heiress of Ballegerno, a child not quite
eleven years of age,—she was recovered by her

friends fifteen days after.—The last case I shall mention is from Fountainhall.—" January 7th, 1688, James Boswell in Kinghorn, brother to Balmuto, is pursued by Anna Carmichael, for ravishing her out of her father's house, and wounding her father, and carrying her to the Queensferry, where she was rescued ; and being absent, he is declared fugitive, whereon his escheat falls."—It may be added, that in Fountainhall's MS. is the following curious notice concerning Lord Stormont, descended from the heiress of Arngosk.—" About this tyme (June 1668,) was given in a bill to the Lords of Secret Counsell complaining on my Lord Stormond, for fraudulent abstracting of Gibson, the Laird of Durie's niece, to whom the custodie of her person in law belongeth ; and for being art and part thereof, by accèssion either antecedent, concomitant, or subsequent.—This bill was given in by Durie, and after a long dispute, the wholle resulting on my Lord Stormond's

oath, he denied all accession thereto, though
it was strongly soupçouned he was not free."

I.

The Highlandmen hae a' come down,
They've a' come down almost,
They've stowen away the bonny lass,
The Lady of Arngosk.

II.

Behind her back they've tied her hands,
An' then they set her on—
" I winna gaug wi' you," she said,
" Nor ony Highland loon."

＊　　＊　　＊　　＊　　＊　　＊　　＊

XXXIV.

Malcolm of Balbedie appears to have been a cadet of the Lochor family, whose representative was created a Baronet of Nova Scotia in the year 1665. "Keep ye weel frae Sir John Malcolm." I do not know the anecdote on which this fragment was composed.

Balbedie has a second son,
  They ca' him Michael Malcolm,
He gangs about Balgonie dykes,
  Huntin' and hawkin';
He's stowen awa' the bonnie lass,
  An' kept the widow wakin'.

XXXV.

The two following Songs allude to some political misfortunes of the Duke of Lauderdale, in the year 1675, which are well known to every reader of history.—Gilbert, is Dr. Burnet, and Margaret, Lady Margaret Kennedy, his wife.

I.

I have been at Newburn, I was in the tower,
I have been in Scotland with a royal power,
I have been with Gilbert, and Marg'ret Kennedy,
But such a huffing parliament did I never see!

II.

Thou shalt get a night-cap and a mourning ring,
And to kepp thy head, thy friends a cloth shall bring,
And in a wooden casement thy head shall be bound,
But thy lusty corpse must stink above the ground.

H

III.

Thou shalt be conducted from Thames to Tweedside
Like a malefactor thy feet shall be tyed,
And from that scurvy process the lawyers shall b
    free,
Thou thought to catch these men, but we have catch
    thee.

———

XXXVI.

I.

Lauderdale, what has become
  Of all thy former huffing,
Has the Commons struck thee dumb
  And sent thee thus a snuffing?
Or is it that the late address
  For removing thee and Bess,
    Does vex thee? &c.

II.

Since the kingdoms thou must quit,
　And seek new habitation,
Will not thy proud Grace think fit
　T'erect a new plantation ?—
And since thou now begins to reel,
　Pray thee go to Old Brazile,
　　And Lord it, &c.

XXXVII.

Sir Robert Laurie, first baronet of the Maxwelton
family (created 27th March 1685,) by his second
wife, a daughter of Riddell of Minto, had three
sons, and four daughters,—of whom Anne was
much celebrated for her beauty, and made a
conquest of Mr. Douglas of Fingland, who is
said to have composed the following verses,—
under an unlucky star,—for the Lady afterwards
married Mr. Ferguson of Craigdarroch.

I.

Maxwelton banks are bonnie,
Whare early fa's the dew;
Whare me and Annie Laurie
Made up the promise true;
Made up the promise true,
And never forget will I,
And for bonnie Annie Laurie
I'd lay down my head and die.

II.

She's backit like a peacock,
She's breastit like a swan,
She's jimp about the middle,
Her waist ye weill may span;
Her waist you weil may span,
And she has a rolling eye,
And for bonnie Annie Laurie
I'd lay down my head and die.

XXXVIII.

TUNE—" How are ye Kimmer."

I.

" Fy, fy, Marg'ret, are ye in ?

' I nae sooner heard it than I did rin,

" Down the gate to tell ye, down the gate to tell ye,

" Down the gate to tell ye, we'll no be left the skin."

II.

" Weel might I kent a' was nae richt,

" For I dreamt o' red and green a' the last nicht ;

" And twa cats fechtin, and twa cats fechtin,

" And twa cats fechtin, I waken'd wi' the fricht."

III.

' Fare ye weel, woman, I maun rin,—

" Trow ye, gif our neighbour Eppie be in,

" And auld Robie Barber, and auld Robie Barber,
" And auld Robie Barber, for I maun tell him."

IV.

" Bide a wee, woman, and gies't a' out,—
" They're bringing in black Papary, I doubt, I doubt,
" And sad reformation, sad reformation,
" Sad reformation in a' the kirks about."

V.

" Mickle do they say, and mair do we hear,
" The Frenches and Irishes are a' coming here,
" And we'll be a' murder'd, murder'd, murder'd,
" We'll a' be murder'd before the new year."

XXXIX.

𝔄 𝔅𝔞𝔩𝔩𝔞𝔡, 𝔟𝔢𝔦𝔫𝔤 𝔱𝔥𝔢 𝔱𝔯𝔲𝔢 𝔠𝔞𝔰𝔢 𝔬𝔣 𝔐𝔯𝔰 𝔈𝔩𝔰𝔭𝔢𝔱, 𝔞 𝔏𝔞𝔡𝔶'𝔰 𝔤𝔢𝔫𝔱𝔩𝔢=𝔴𝔬𝔪𝔞𝔫, 𝔫𝔢𝔞𝔯 𝔈𝔡𝔦𝔫𝔟𝔲𝔯𝔤𝔥.

This and the following Ballad were written by Charles Lord Binning, who died in the life-time of his father, the Earl of Haddington, 1733.—See Park's edition of Walpole's Royal and Noble Authors, vol. 5th.

I.

Lang hae I lo'ed the blate Mass John,
   And sair my breast has smarted,
I never saw a Dominie
   Was half sae cruel hearted !

II.

With pleasing words I feast his ears,
  With dainty food I fill him ;
I would not take the Chamberlain,
  But that did naething till him !

III.

When he was with the tooth-ache fash'd,
  I bled his gums with leeches,—
To keep him warm, I sewed mysel',
  Three buttons on his breeches.

IV.

I lo'e him in a lawful way,
  No lawful love is wicked :
I ne'er set on the succar pan,
  But he got aye a lick o't.

V.

Whene'er my dearie would come in,
  The door was never lockit,
Nor wanted he for a la creesh,
  And seed-cake in his pocket.

VI.

I cut the phlegm with Athole brose,
   When cauld did quite confound him;
I gave him wangrace in his bed,
   And row'd the blankets round him.

VII.

With darning his auld coarsest sarks,
   I scarce have left a thumb on ;
But sae I should, for chaplains used
   To love the gentlewoman.

VIII.

But tho' he reads the Bible book,
   It makes but sma' impression ;
Indeed, he catch'd the cook with Kate,
   And sent them to the Session.

IX.

They did not well in what they did,
   So ill the matter ended ;
But lawful love's another thing,
   And ought to be commended.

X.

With comfort meet we should delight,
  Mankind should not miscarry;
But he, for all that I can do,
  Will neither burn nor marry.

XI.

Hoot, fye for shame—be brisk Mass John,
  Ye look as ye were sleepin';
Ye craw not like a stately fowl,
  But cackle like a capon.

XII.

Oh, dour Mass John—Oh, dreigh Mass John,
  When I have told you sae far!
A shame light on your loggerhead,
  Ye doited, donnart, duffar!

XL.

TUNE—" O London is a Fine Town."

I.

Was ever dame in such distress ?
  My heart is full of care ;
Such various plagues torment my mind,
  That I am in despair.

II.

I'm on, and off, and off and on,
  And know not what to do ;
I have a cook to dress my meat,
  But I want to get me two.

III.

This cook a handy damsel is,
    And dresses very weel;
Her kitchen is as clean's her face,
    And her pewther shines like steel.

IV.

But she has no experience,
    And has so little seen,
That when I want variety,
    She kills me with the spleen.

V.

I have a man cook in my view,
    To help her out a dish,
That when she is employ'd with meat,
    The lad may dress the fish.

VI.

But then the lad a head cook is,
    And second will not be;
I must pack off the lass, I fear,
    For I cant afford her fee.

VII.

But then the lass has done no fault,—
　I'll keep her, I'm resolved,—
I'll get the man to give her half,
　And so the doubt is solv'd.

VIII.

But what if they should not agree,—
　They will my victuals spoil ;
He'll say 'tis her, and she 'tis him,
　And plague me with turmoil.

IX.

I'll not have him, and part with her,
　And yet I'll have him too ;
I'll part with her—no, no, I wont,—
　O Stars, what shall I do ?

XLI.

The two following Songs were composed by Annie, daughter of Sir James Mackenzie, Bart. a Senator of the College of Justice, bearing the title of Lord Royston ; she is said to have inherited the wit of her grand-fathers, the first Earl of Cromarty, and Sir George Mackenzie of Rosehaugh, which in some cases overbalanced her discretion,—her lampoons excited as much hatred as mirth,—and she met with those spiteful returns which such poetesses must ever expect. This lively Lady had no children by her husband, Sir William Dick of Prestonfield, Bart. and died in the year 1741.—Her Phaon, whom she seems to laugh at in these verses, was Sir Patrick Murray of Balmanno.

1.

Oh, wherefor did I cross the Forth,
 And leave my love behind me,
Why did I venture to the north,
 With one that does not mind me ?

II.

Had I but visited Carin!
   It would have been much better,
Than pique the prudes, and make a din,
   For careless, cold Sir Peter!

III.

I'm sure I've seen a better limb,
   And twenty better faces;
But still my mind it ran on him,
   When I was at the races.

IV.

At night when we went to the ball,
   Were many there discreeter;
The well-bred Duke, * and lively Maule,
   Panmure behav'd much better.

V.

They kindly show'd their courtesy,
   And look'd on me much sweeter,
Yet easy could I never be,
   For thinking on Sir Peter.

---

    * The Duke of Hamilton.

VI.

I fain would wear an easy air,
  But oh ! it look'd affected ;
And e'en the fine ambassador, *
  Could see he was neglected.

VII.

Tho' Poury left for me the spleen,
  My temper grew no sweeter,
I think I'm mad,—what do I mean,
  To follow cold Sir Peter ! ! !

---

* The Earl of Stair.

XLII.

Written after a Raffle, in which Sir Patrick gained
a Fan and a Snuff Box.—English Margaret was
Lady Margaret Montgomerie, daughter to the
Earl of Eglintoune, and afterwards the wife of
Sir James Macdonald of Slate.—She is termed
English, because she was educated at a boarding
school near London.

I.

What charms can English Margaret boast,
   To fix thy inconstant mind,
And keep the heart that I have lost?
   O cruel and unkind!

I

II.

For I cau kilt my coats us high,
  And curl my red toupee—
And I'll put on the English mutch
  If that has charms for thee.

III.

Let no nymph toss thy leathern fan,
  Nor damsel touch thy box ;
For I'll, Balmanno, have thee all,
  Even take thee with a * * * !

IV.

Since that's, alas, thy woful case,
  There's none so fit as I ;
For ne'er a lass in all the land,
  Can boast more mercury.

XLIII.

Mrs Mitchel and Borlan.

From circumstances I suspect this Song to be the composition of Lady Dick, but am not certain.

I.

" Who's that at my chamber door?"
    " It's I, my dear," quo' Borlan,—
" Come in," quo' she, " let's chat a while,
    " You strapping sturdy Norlan!"

II.

Fair Mitchell needed add no more,
    For Borlan straight did enter,
And on his knees he vow'd and swore,
    For her he all would venture.

III.

Fair Mitchell answer'd with a blush,
  " Your love I dont mistrust, Sir,
" But should it reach my father's ear,
  " How would he puff and bluster !"

IV.

" O, let him bluster as he will,"
  Replied the amorous lover,
" If you'll consent my arms to fill,
  " Let him go to Hanover."

THE END.

Webster, Printer, Horse Wynd.

A

North Countrie

Garland.

Edinburgh.

MDCCCXXIV.

𝔓𝔯𝔢𝔣𝔞𝔠𝔢.

HE BALLADS collected in this present little Volume, have, with one solitary exception, been for the first time printed.

'Lord Thomas Stuart,'—'The burning of 'Frendraught,' — 'Child Vyet,' — 'Bonny 'John Seton,'—and two or three others, of minor importance, had long been preserved by tradition, in Aberdeenshire; and were procured from an intelligent individual, resident in that part of Scotland.

'The Jolly Hawk,'—from the pen of the amiable Lord Binning, was originally printed in a Collection of Songs, ('The Charmer,') Edinburgh, 1751, 2 vols. 12mo. The uncom-

mon occurrence of this work, and the clever-
ness of the Song itself, was the cause of its
insertion here.

The sources, from which the other Ballads
were obtained, have been for the most part
mentioned, in the notice, prefixed to each
Song.

Whatever other merit, this ' NORTH
' COUNTRIE GARLAND,' may have, it
must be allowed, to possess that of *rarity :*
(THIRTY COPIES only having been printed,
chiefly for the gratification of a few of the
Editor's Friends,)—a circumstance of itself,
quite sufficient to give it value in the eyes of
Bibliomaniacs.

EDINBURGH, }
17th February 1824.}

CONTENTS.

Lord Thomas Stuart.

With the circumstances which have given rise to
this Ballad, the Editor is unacquainted.

I.

Thomas Stuart was a Lord,
   A Lord of mickle land,
He used to wear a coat of gold,
   But now his grave is green.

II.

Now he has wooed the young Countess,
   The Countess of Balquhin,
An' given her for a morning gift,
   Strathboggie and Aboyne.

III.

But women's wit is aye willful,
   Alas! that ever it was sae,
She longed to see the morning gift,
   That her gude Lord to her gae.

IV.

When steeds were saddled, an' weel bridled,
   An' ready for to ride,
There came a pain on that gude Lord,
   His back likewise his side.

V.

He said, " ride on my Lady fair,
   " May goodness be your guide,
" For I'm sae sick an' weary, that
   " No farther can I ride."

VI.

Now ben did come his father dear,
   Wearing a golden band,
Says, " is there nae leech in Edinburgh,
   " Can cure my son from wrang."

VII.

" O leech is come, au' leech is gane,
   " Yet father I'm aye waur,
" There's not a leech in Edinbro'
   " Can death from me debar.

VIII.

" But be a friend to my wife, father,
   " Restore to her her own,
" Restore to her my morning gift,
   " Strathboggie and Aboyne.

IX.

" It had been gude for my wife, father,
   " To me she'd born a son,
" He would have got my land an' rents,
   " Where they lie out an' in.

X.

" It had been gude for my wife, father,
    " To me she'd born an heir,
" He would have got my land an' rents,
    " Where they lie fine an' fair."

XI.

The steeds they strave into their stables,
    The boys could'nt get them bound,
The hounds lay howling on the leech,
    'Cause their master was behind,

XII.

I dreamed a dream since late yestreen,
    I wish it may be good,
That our chamber was full of swine,
    An' our bed full of blood,

XIII.

I saw a woman come from the west,
    Full sore wringing her hands,
And aye she cried, " Ohon, alas !
    " My good Lord's broken bands."

XIV.

As she came by my good Lord's bower,
    Saw mony black steeds an' brown,
" I'm feared it be mony unco Lords
    " Havin' my love from town."

XV.

As she came by my gude Lord's bower,
  Saw mony black steeds an' grey,
" I'm feared it's mony unco Lords
" Havin' my love to the clay."

Burning of Frendraught.

This Ballad, which possesses considerable merit,
  was supposed by Ritson to have been lost.—A
  full account of the circumstances which gave
  rise to it will be found in Spalding, Vol. I. p. 9.

I.

The eighteenth day of October,
  A dismal tale to hear,
How good Lord John an' Rothiemay,
  Were both burnt in the fire.

II.

When steeds were saddled an' well bridled,
  And ready for to ride,
Then out there came the false Frendraught,
  Inviting them to bide.

III.

Said, stay this night until we sup,
  " The morn until we dine,
" 'Twill be token of good 'greement,
  " 'Twixt your good Lord an' mine."

IV.

" We'll turn again," said good Lord John,
  " But, no !" said Rothiemay,
" My steed's trapanned, my bridle's broken,
  " I fear the day I'm fay."

V.

When mass was sung, and bells were rung,
  And all men bound for bed,
Then good Lord John and Rothiemay,
  In one chamber were laid.

VI.

They had not long cast off their clothes,
  And were but new asleep,
When weary smoke began to rise,
  Likewise the scorching heat.

VII.

" O waken, waken, Rothiemay,
  " O waken, brother dear,
" And turn you to your Saviour,
  " There is strong treason here."

VIII.

When they were dressed wi' their clothes,
    An' ready for to boun',
The doors and windows were all secured,
    The roof tree burning doun.

IX.

He did flee to the wire window,
    As fast as he could gang,
Says, " woe to the hands put in the stanchions,
    " For out we'll never win."

X.

While he stood at the wire window,
    Most doleful to be seen,
He did espy the Lady Frendraught,
    Who stood upon the green,

XI.

" Mercy ! mercy ! Lady Frendraught,
    " Will ye not sink with sin,
" For first your husband kill'd my father,
    " And now you burn his son."

XII.

O then out spake the Lady Frendraught,
    And loudly did she cry :
" It were great pity for good Lord John,
    " But none for Rothiemay ;
" The keys were casten in the deep draw well,
    " Ye cannot win away."

XIII.

While he stood in this dreadful plight,
    Most piteous to be seen,
Then called out his servant Gordon,
    As he had frantic been.

XIV.

" O loup ! O loup ! my dear master,
    " O loup and come to me,
" I'll catch you in my arms two,
    " One foot I will not flee.

XV.

" O loup ! O loup ! my dear master,
    " O loup and come away,
" I'll catch you in my arms two,
    " But Rothiemay may lay."

XVI.

" The fish shall ne'er swim in the flood,
    " Nor corn grow thro' the clay,
" Nor the fiercest fire that ere was kindled,
    " Twin me and Rothiemay.

XVII.

" I cannot loup, I cannot come,
    " I cannot win to thee,
" My head's fast in the wire window,
    My feet burning from me.

K

XVIII.

" My eyes are southering in my head,
  " My flesh roasting also,
" My bowels are boiling with my blood,
  " Is not that a woeful woe?

XIX.

" Take here the rings from my white fingers,
  " Which are so long and small,
" And give them to my Lady fair,
  " Where she sits in her hall.

XX.

" I cannot loup, I cannot come,
  " I cannot loup to thee,
" My earthly part is all consum'd,
  " My spirit speaks to thee."

XXI.

Wringing her hands, tearing her hair,
  His lady fair was seen,
Calling unto his servant Gordon,
  Where he stood on the green.

XXII.

" O woe be to you, George Gordon,
  " An ill death may you dee,
" So safe and sound as you stand there,
  " And my Lord burned from me."

XXIII.

" I bade him loup, I bade him come,
  " I bade him come to me ;
" I'd catch him in my arms two,
  " A foot I would not flee.

XXIV.

" He threw me the rings from his white fingers,
  " Which are so long and small,
" To give to you, his Lady fair,
  " Where you sit in your hall."

XXV.

Sophia Hay, Sophia Hay,
  Bonny Sophia, was her name;
Her waiting maid put on her clothes,
  But she tore them off again.

XXVI.

And oft she cried, " Ohon, alas !
  " A sair heart's easy wan,
" I wan a sair heart when I married him,
  " The day it's returned again." *

---

* For farther particulars regarding this disastrous
event, see Gordon's History of the Family of Gordon, Vol. II. p. 138.—The Genealogical History
of the Family of Sutherland, p. 420. — Ritson's
Scotish Ballads, Vol. II. p. 31, and Finlay's Ballads, Vol. I. p. 59.

Lord Salton and Auchanachie.

The circumstances which gave rise to this Ballad
are unknown to the Editor.

———————————

*　　*　　*　　*　　*

I.

Ben came her father,
　Skipping on the floor,
Said, " Jeanie, your trying
　" The tricks of a whore.

II.

" You're caring for him,
　" That cares not for thee,
" And I pray you take Salton,
　" Let Auchanachie be."

III.

" I will not have Salton,
　" It lies low by the sea ;
" He is bowed in the back,
　" He's thrawen in the knee,
" And I'll die if I get not
　" My brave Auchanachie."

IV.

" I am bowed in the back,
   " Lassie as ye see,
" But the bonny lands of Salton,
   " Are no crooked tee."

V.

And when she was married,
   She would not lie down,
But they took out a knife,
   And cuttit her gown;

VI.

Likewise of her stays,
   The lacing in three,
And now she lies dead,
   For her Auchanachie.

VII.

Out comes her bower woman,
   Wringing her hands,
Says, " alas! for the staying
   " So long on the sands.

VIII.

" Alas! for the staying
   " So long on the flood,
" For Jeanie was married,
   " And now she is dead."

The Young Laird of Craigstoun.

The estate of Craigstoun was acquired by John Urquhart, better known by the name of the Tutor of Cromarty. It would appear, that the Ballad refers to his grand-son, who married Elizabeth, daughter of Sir Robert Innes of that Ilk, and by her had one son. This John Urquhart died 30th November 1634.—Spalding, (vol. I. p. 36,) after mentioning the great mortality in the Craigstoun family says, "thus in three years space, the good-sire, son, and oy, died," He adds, that " the Laird of Innes, (whose sister was married to this Urquhart of Leathers, (the father,) and not without her consent, as was thought, gets the guiding of this *young boy*, and without advice of friends, shortly and quietly marries him, upon his own eldest daughter Elizabeth Innes." He mentions, that young Craigstoun's death was generally attributed to melancholy, in consequence of Sir Robert Innes refusing to pay old Craigstoun's debts. The creditors bestowing " many maledictions, which touched the young man's conscience, albeit he could not mend it." The father died in December 1631, and the son in 1634. The marriage consequently must have been of short duration.

I.

" Father," said she, " you have done me wrong,
" For ye have married me, on a childe young man,
" For ye have married me, on a childe young man,
" And my bonny love is long
    " A growing, growing, deary,
     " Growing, growing, said the bonny maid,
     " How long my bonny love's growing."

II.

" Daughter," said he, " I have done you no wrong,
" For I have married you on a heritor of lan',
" He's likewise possessed of many bills and bonds,
" And he'll be daily
    " Growing, growing, deary," &c.

III.

" Daughter," said he, " if ye wish to do well,
" Ye will send your husband away to the school,
" That he of learning may gather great skill,
" And he'll be daily
    " Growing, growing," &c.

IV.

Now young Craigstoun to the college is gone,
And left his Lady making great moan,
That she should be forced to lie a-bed alone,
And that he was so long
    A growing, growing, &c.

V.

She's dressed herself in robes of green,
They were right comely to be seen,
She was the picture of Venus' queen,
And she's to the college to see
    Him growing, growing, &c.

VI.

Then all the Collegiuers were playing at the ba',
But the young Craigstoun was the flower of them a';
He said, " play on my school-fellows a',
" For I see my sister
    " Coming, coming," &c.

VII.

Now down into the college park,
They walked about till it was dark,
Then he lifted up her fine Holland sark,
And she had no reason to complain
    Of his growing, growing, &c.

VIII.

In his twelfth year, he was a married man,
In his thirteenth year, then he got a son; *
And in his fourteenth year, his grave grew green,
And that was an end
    Of his growing, growing, &c.

---

   * By the extinction of the elder branch of the
family, this son succeeded to the estate of Cromarty.

Bonny John Seton.

John Seton of Pitmeddin, is said by Douglas, in
his Baronage, (p. 182) to have been " a man of
good natural parts, which were greatly improv-
ed by a liberal education and travelling." He
was a steady loyalist, and having repaired to
the Earl of Aboyne's standard, commanded a
detachment of the Cavalier's at the battle of
the Bridge of Dee, where he was unfortunately
shot through the heart with a cannon ball, with
the royal standard in his hand, June 1639, in
the 29th year of his age. He was father of that
celebrated lawyer Sir Alexander Seton, Bart. of
Pitmeddin.

I.

Upon the eighteenth day of June,
  A dreary day to see,
The Southern Lords did pitch their camp,
  Just at the Bridge of Dee.

II.

Bonny John Seton of Pitmeddin,
  A bold baron was he,
He made his testament ere he went out,
  The wiser man was he.

III.

He left his land to his young son,
   His Lady her dowry,
A thousand crowns to his daughter Jean,
   Yet on the nurse's knee.

IV.

Then out came his Lady fair,
   A tear into her e'e,
Says, " stay at home, my own good Lord,
   " O! stay at home with me."

V.

He looked over his left shoulder,
   Cried, " souldiers follow me !"
O! then she looked in his face,
   An angry woman was she;
" God send me back my steed again,
   " But ne'er let me see thee."

VI.

His name was Major Middleton,
   That manned the Bridge of Dee ;
His name was Colonel Henderson,
   That let the cannons flee.

VII.

His name was Major Middleton,
   That manned the Bridge of Dee,
And his name was Colonel Henderson,
   That dung Pitmeddin in three.

VIII.

Some rode on the black and grey,
  And some rode on the brown ;
But the bonny John Seton,
  Lay gasping on the ground.

IX.

Then bye there comes a false Forbes,
  Was riding from Driminere,
Says, " here there lies a proud Seton,
  " This day they ride the rear."

X.

Craigievar said to his men,
  " You may play on your shield,
" For the proudest Seton in all the lan',
  " This day lies on the field.

XI.

" O spoil him ! spoil him !" cried Craigievar,
  " Him spoiled let me see,
" For on my word," said Craigievar,
  " He had no good will at me."

XII.

They took from him his armour clear,
  His sword, likewise his shield ;
Yea, they have left him naked there,
  Upon the open field.

XIII.

The Highland men, they're clever men,
    At handling sword and shield,
But yet they are too naked men,
    To stay in battle field.

XIV.

The Highland men, are clever men,
    At handling sword or gun,
But yet they are too naked men,
    To bear the cannon's rung.

XV.

For a cannon's roar, in a summer night,
    Is like thunder in the air,
There's not a man in Highland dress,
    Can face the cannon's fire. *

---

* William Forbes of Craigievar, was, by Charles I. created a Baronet of Nova Scotia, by patent dated 20th April 1630.—He took an active part on the side of the Parliament, and was made Sheriff of Aberdeen, (1647) and one of the Commissioners for selling the estates of the " malignants."

Mary Hamilton.

In the Border Minstrelsy, there occurs another Ballad on the same subject, "The Queen's Marie." A notice is prefixed, to which reference is made. The present Ballad differs considerably from that preserved by Sir Walter Scott, and appears to be a fragment.

I.

Then down cam Queen Marie,
   Wi' gold links in her hair,
Saying, " Marie mild, where is the child,
   " That I heard greet sae sair ?"

II.

" There was nae child wi' me madam,
   " There was nae child wi' me,
" It was but me in a sair cholic,
   " When I was like to die !"

III.

" I'm not deceived," Queen Marie said,
   " No, no, indeed ! not I !
" So Marie mild, where is the child ?
   " For sure I heard it cry."

IV.

She turned down the blankets fine,
   Likewise the Holland sheet,
And underneath, there strangled lay,
   A lovely Baby sweet.

V.

" O cruel mother !" said the Queen,
   " Some fiend possessed thee,
" But I will hang thee for this deed,
   " My Marie tho' thou be !"

*   *   *   *   *

VI.

When she cam to the Nether-Bow Port,
   She laugh't loud laughters three;
But when she cam to the gallows foot,
   The saut tear blinded her e'e.

VII.

" Yestreen the Queen had four Maries,
   " The night she'll hae but three ;
" There was Marie Seton, and Marie Beaton,
   " And Marie Carmichael and me.

VIII.

" Ye mariners, ye mariners,
   " That sail upon the see,
" Let not my father or mother wit,
   " The death that I maun die.

IX.

" I was my parents' only hope,

" They ne'er had ane but me,

" They little thought when I left hame,

" They should nae mair me see !"

Burd Ellen and Young Tamlane.

The following fragment was communicated to the Editor, by his friend R. Pitcairn, Esq. who took it down from the recitation of a female relative, who had heard it frequently sung in her childhood about sixty years since. To that gentleman he is indebted for the following notice :—

" *Burd Ellen*, referred to in the following fragment, is the *Proud Eline*, of the northren minstrels; the *Burd Ellen* of the Scots; *La Prude Dame Eline*, of the French; and the *Gentle Lady Eline*, of the English. The term *Prud*, which was afterwards corrupted into *Burd*, is equally applicable to Knights, as well as to Ladies, in the Danish, Swedish, and French languages. The *Ritter Hin Prud* of the Danish, the *Preux Chevalier* of the French and the *Gentle Knight* of the English ballads and romances, are identically the same.

" *Young Tamlane,* in like manner, is a very popular personage, in our romantic ballads, and appears under the variations of *Thom of Lynn, Thom-a-Lin, Tomlin,* and *Tom Linn,* &c. Reference may be made to the Border Minstrelsy, where the *Tale of Tamlane* is prefaced by a very valuable dissertation, on the fairies of popular superstition ; and also to Jamieson's Collection, for many interesting particulars.

" It is highly probable, that Burd Ellen, &c. may be a popular corruption of *Burd-alayn,* or *Burdalane,* which signifies an only child, a maiden," &c.

1.

Burd Ellen sits in her bower windowe,
 With a double laddy double, and for the double dow,
Twisting the red silk and the blue,
 With the double rose and the May-hay.

II.

And whiles she twisted, and whiles she twan,
 With a double, &c.
And whiles the tears fell down amang,
 With the double, &c.

III.

Till once there by cam Young Tamlane,
   With a double, &c.
" Come light, oh light, and rock your young son !"
   With the double, &c.

IV.

" If you winna rock him, you may let him rair,
   " With a double, &c.
" For I hae rockit my share and mair !
   " With the double," &c.
     *   *   *   *   *

V.

Young Tamlane to the seas he's gane,
   With a double laddy double, and for the double dow,
And a' women's curse in his company's gane !
   With the double rose and the May-hay.

Child Vyet.

Mr Jamieson, in his Ballads, Vol. II. page 265,
has published from Mr. Herd's MS. " Lord
. Wa'yates and auld Ingram," in which the story
very much resembles what occurs here. The
versification of it is totally different. " Lord
Wa'yates " is, however, a fragment, and the ca-
tastrophe is wanting.—This deficiency is fortunately supplied by the present Ballad.

I.

Lord Ingram and Childe Vyet,
  Were both born in ane bower,
Had both their loves on one Lady,
  The loss was their honour.

II.

Childe Vyet and Lord Ingram,
  Were both born in one hall,
Had both their loves on one Lady,
  The worse did them befall.

III.

Lord Ingram woo'd the Lady Maiserey,
  From father and from mother ;
Lord Ingram woo'd the Lady Maiserey,
  From sister and from brother.

IV.

Lord Ingram wooed the Lady Maiserey,
    With leave of all her kin ;
And every one gave full consent,
    But she said " No," to him.

V.

Lord Ingram wooed the Lady Maiserey,
    Into her father's ha' ;
Childe Vyet wooed the Lady Maiserey,
    Among the sheets so sma'.

VI.

Now it fell out upon a day,
    She was dressing her head,
That ben did come her father dear,
    Wearing the gold so red.

VII.

" Get up now Lady Maiserey,
    " Put on your wedding gown,
" For Lord Ingram will be here,
    " Your wedding must be done !"

VIII.

" I'd rather be Childe Vyet's wife,
    " The white fish for to sell,
" Before I were Lord Iugram's wife,
    " To wear the silk so well !

IX.

" I'd rather be Childe Vyet's wife,
  " With him to beg my bread,
" Before I'd be Lord Ingram's wife,
  " To wear the gold so red.

X.

" Where will I get a bonny boy,
  " Will win gold to his fee,
" Will run unto Childe Vyet's ha',
  " With this letter from me ?

XI.

" O here, I am the boy," says one,
  " Will win gold to my fee,
" And carry away any letter,
  " To Childe Vyet from thee."

XII.

And when he found the bridges broke,
  He bent his bow and swam,
And when he found the grass growing,
  He hasten'd and he ran.

XIII.

And when he came to Vyet's castle,
  He did not knock nor call,
But set his bent bow to his breast,
  And lightly leaped the wall ;
And ere the porter open'd the gate,
  The boy was in the hall.

XIV.

The first line that Childe Vyet read,
  A. grieved man was he;
The next line that he looked on,
  A tear blinded his e'e.

XV.

" What ails my one brother," he says,
  " He'll not let my love be,
" But I'll send to my brother's bridal,
  " The woman shall be free.

XVI.

" Take four and twenty bucks and ewes,
  " And ten tun of the wine,
" And bid my love be blythe and glad,
  " And I will follow syne."

XVII.

There was not a groom about that castle,
  But got a gown of green;
And a' was blythe, and a' was glad,
  But Lady Maiserey was wi' wean.

XVIII.

There was no cook about the kitchen,
  But got a gown of gray,
And a' was blythe, and a' was glad,
  But Lady Maiserey was wae.

XIX.

'Tween Marykirk and that castle,
　Was all spread o'er with gold,
To keep the Lady and her maidens,
　From tramping on the mould.

XX.

From Marykirk to that castle,
　Was spread a cloth of gold,
To keep the Lady and her maidens,
　From treading on the mould.

XXI.

When mass was sung, and bells were rung,
　And all men bound for bed,
Then Lord Ingram and Lady Maiserey,
　In one bed they were laid.

XXII.

When they were laid upon their bed,
　It was baith soft and warm,
He laid his hand over her side,
　Says he, " you are with bairn."

XXIII.

" I told you once, so did I twice.
　" When ye came as my wooer,
" That Childe Vyet, your one brother,
　'" One night lay in my bower.

XXIV.

" I told you twice, so did I thrice,
   " Ere ye came me to wed,
" That Childe Vyet, your one brother,
   " One night lay in my bed !"

XXV.

" O will you father your bairn on me,
   " And on no other man,
" And I'll gie him to his dowry,
   " Full fifty ploughs of land ?"

XXVI.

" I will not father my bairn on you,
   " Nor on no wrongous man,
" Tho' you'd gie him to his dowry,
   " Five thousand ploughs of land."

XXVII.

Then up did start him Childe Vyet,
   Shed by his yellow hair,
And gave Lord Ingram to the heart,
   A deep wouud and a sair.

XXVIII.

Then up did start him Lord Ingram,
   Shed by his yellow hair,
And gave Childe Vyet to the heart,
   A deep wound and a sair.

XXIX.

There was no pity for the two Lords,
  When they were lying slain,
All was for Lady Maiserey,
  In that bower she gaed brain !

XXX.

There was no pity for the two Lords,
  When they were lying dead,
All was for Lady Maiserey,
  In that bower she went mad !

XXXI.

" O get to me a cloak of cloth,
  " A staff of good hard tree,
" If I have been an evil woman,
  · " I shall beg till I die.

XXXII.

" For ae bit I'll beg for Childe Vyet,
  " For Lord Ingram I'll beg three,
" All for the honourable marriage, that
  " At Marykirk he gave me !"

Errol's Place.

Gilbert, who succeeded in the year 1636, to the
Earldom of Errol, and who married Catherine,
daughter of James, second Earl of Southesque
is the hero of this strange song.—He died without issue, anno 1674.—There is a *south-country*
Ballad on the same subject, which is considerably longer, and in which the incidents vary
materially; particularly, Lady Errol tries to
poison her husband, an attempt passed over in
silence in the present copy, which is the *north-
country* version of the story.

I.

O Errol's place, is a bonny place,
    It stands upon yon plain,
The flowers at it grow red and white,
    The apples red and green.
Chorus.
    The wally o't, the wally o't,
      According as you ken,
    The thing they ca' the ranting o't,
      Our lady lies alane !

II.

O Errol's place, is a bonny place,
  It stands upon yon plain,
But what's the use of Errol's place,
  He's no like other men?
    · The wally, &c.

III.

" It's I cam in by yon canal,
  " And by yon bowling green,
I might have pleased the best Carnegie,
  " That ever bore that name."
    The wally, &c.

IV.

" As sure as your Jean Carnegie,
  " And I am Gibbie Hay,
" I'll cause your father to sell his land,
  " Your tocher for to pay."
    The wally, &c.

V.

" To cause my father to sell his land,
  " I think would be a sin,
" To give to such a rogue as you,
  " Who never could it win !"
    The wally, &c.

VI.

So he must go to Edinburgh,
  Amang the nobles a',
And there before good witnesses,
  His manhood for to shaw.
    The wally, &c.

VII.

Then out it's spoke her sister,
  Whose name was called Miss Ann,
" Had I been Lady Errol,
  " Or come of sic a clan,
" I would not in this public way.
  " Have sham'd my own gude man."
    The wally, &c.

VIII.

A servant girl there was found out,
  On whom to shew his skill,
He gave to her a hundred pounds,
  To purchase her good will.
    The wally, &c.

IX.

And still he cried, " look up Peggy,
  " Look up and think no shame,
" And you shall have your hundred pounds,
  " Before I lay you down."
    The wally, &c.

X.

Now he has lain him down wi' her,
  A hundred pounds in pawn,
And all the noblemen cried out,
  " That Errol is a man."
    The wally, &c.

XI.

" Tak hame your daughter," Errol said,
  " And tak her to a glen,
" For Errol canna pleasure her,
  " Nor can no other man."
    The wally, &c.

Catharine Jaffery.

In the Border Minstrelsy, occurs another version
of Catharine Jaffery, much superior to the present one in poetical merit.—As a north country
Edition of a Border Ballad, the Editor has, however, been induced to preserve it.

I.

O bonny Catharine Jaffery,
  That dainty maid so fair,
Once lov'd the laird of Lochinvar,
  Without any compare.

II.

'Long time she loo'd him very well,
　　But they changed her mind away,
And now she goes another's bride,
　　And plays him foul play.

III.

The bonny Laird of Lauderdale,
　　Came from the south·countrie,
And he has wooed the pretty maid,
　　Thro' presents entered he.

IV.

For tocher gear, he did not stand,
　　She was a dainty May,
He 'greed him with her friends all,
　　And set the wedding day.

V.

When Lochinvar got word of this,
　　He knew not what to do,
For losing of a lady fair,
　　That he did love so true.

VI.

But 'if I were young Lochinvar,
　　I wou'd not care a fly,
To take her on her wedding day,
　　From all her company.

VII.

Get ye a quiet messenger,
  Send him thro' all your land,
For a hundred and fifty brave young lads,
  To be at your command.

VIII.

To be all at your command,
  And your bidding to obey,
Yet still cause you the trumpet sound,
  The voice of foul play.

IX.

He got a quiet messenger,
  To send thro' all his land,
And full three hundred pretty lads,
  Were all at his command.

X.

Were all at his command,
  And his bidding did obey,
Yet still he made the trumpet sound,
  The voice of foul play.

XI.

Then he went to the bridal house,
  Among the nobles a',
And when he stepped upon the floor,
  He gave a loud huzza !

XII.

" Huzza ! Huzza ! you English men,
  " Or Borderers who were born,
" Ne'er come to Scotland for a maid,
  Or else they will you scorn.

XIII.

" She'll bring yòu on with tempting words,
  " Aye, 'till the wedding day.
" Syne give you frogs instead of fish,
  " And play you foul play."

XIV.

The gentlemen all wondered,
  What could be in his mind,
And asked " if he'd a mind to fight,
  " Why spoke he so unkind ?

XV.

" Did he e'er see such pretty men,
  " As were there in array ?"
" O yes," said he, " a fairy court,
  " Were leaping on the hay.

XVI.

" As I came in by Hyland banks,
  " And in by Hyland braes,
" There did I see a fairy court,
  " All leaping on the leas.

XVII.

" I came not here to fight," he said,
  " But for good fellowship gay ;
" I want to drink with your bridegroom,
  " And then I'll boun' my way."

XVIII.

The glass was filled with good red wine,
  And drunk between them twae ;
" Give me one shake of your bonny bride's hand,
  And then I'll boun' my way."

XIX.

He's ta'en her by the milk-white hands,
  And by the grass green sleeve,
Pull'd her on horse back him behind,
  At her friends ask'd nae leave.

XX.

Syne rode the water with great speed,
  And merrily the knows,
Then fifty from the bridal came,
  Indeed it was nae mows.

XXI.

Thinking to take the bride again.
  Thro' strength if that they may,
But still he gar't the trumpet sound,
  The voice of foul play.

XXII.

There were four and twenty ladies fair,
   All walking on the lea,
He gave to them the bonny bride,
   And bade them boun' their way.

XXIII.

They splintered the spears in pieces now,
   And the blades flew in the sky,
But the bonny Laird of Lochinvar,
   Has gained the victory.

XXIV.

Many a wife and widow's son,
   Lay gasping on the ground,
But the bonny Laird of Lochinvar,
   He has the victory won.

Eppie Morrie.

This Ballad is probably much more than a century
old, though the circumstances which have given
rise to it were unfortunately too common to
preclude the possibility of its being of a later
date.—Although evidently founded on fact, the
Editor has not hitherto discovered the particular circumstances out of which it has originated.

I.

Four and twenty Highland men,
　Came a' from Carrie side,
To steal awa' Eppie Morrie,
　'Cause she would not be a bride.

II.

Out it's came her mother,
　It was a moonlight night,
She could not see her daughter,
　There swords they shin'd so bright.

III.

" Haud far awa' frae me mother,
　" Haud far awa' frae me,
" There's not a man in a' Strathdon,
　" Shall wedded be with me."

IV.

They have taken Eppie Morrie,
   And horse back bound her on,
And then awa' to the miuister,
   As fast as horse could gang.

V.

He's taken out a pistol, and
   Set it to the minister's breast ;
" Marry me, marry me, minister,
   " Or else I'll be your priest."

VI.

" Haud far awa' frae me, good Sir,
   " Haud far awa' frae me,
" For there's not a man in all Strathdon,
   " That shall married be with me. "

VII.

" Haud far awa' frae me, Willie,
   " Haud far awa' frae me,
" For I darna avow to marry you,
   " Except she's as willing as ye."

VIII.

They have taken Eppie Morrie,
   Since better could nae be,
And they're awa' to Carrie side,
   As fast as horse could flee.

IX.

When mass was sung, and bells were rung,
    And all were bound for bed,
Then Willie an' Eppie Morrie,
    In one bed they were laid.

X.

" Haud far awa' frae me, Willie,
    " Haud far awa' frae me,
" Before I lose my maidenhead,
    " I'll try my strength with thee."

XI.

She took the cap from off her head,
    And threw it to the way,
Said, " ere I lose my maidenhead,
    " I'll fight with you till day."

XII.

Then early in the morning,
    Before her clothes were on,
In came the maiden of Scalletter,
    Gown and shirt alone.

XIII.

" Get up, get up, young woman,
    " And drink the wine wi' me :"
" Ye might have called me maiden,
    " I'm sure as leal as thee "

XIV.

" Wally fa' you, Willie, that
" Ye could nae prove a man,
" And taen the lassie's maidenhead,
" She would have hired your han'."

XV.

" Haud far awa' frae me, lady,
" Haud far awa' frae me,
" There's not a man in a' Strathdon,
" The day shall wed wi' me."

XVI.

Soon in there came Belbordlane,
With a pistol on every side,
" Came awa' hame Eppie Morrie,
" And there you'll be my bride."

XVII.

" Go get to me a horse, Willie,
" And get it like a man,
" And send me back to my mother,
" A maiden as I cam."

XVIII.

The sun shines o'er the westlin hills,
By the light lamp of the moon,
Just saddle your horse, young John Forsyth,
And whistle and I'll come soon.

Rob Roy M'Gregor.

From a MS. Collection of Ballads, &c. in the possession of R. Pitcairn, Esq., who notes, that he took it from the recitation of Widow Stevenson. The First Part is sung to the air of " The Bonny House of Airley ;" and the latter Part, " Haud awa' frae me, Donald:"—It forms an appropriate sequel to Eppie Morrie.

I.

Rob Roy from the Highlands cam,
  Unto our Scottish border,
And he has stow'n a lady fair,
  To haud his house in order.

II.

And when he cam, he surrounded the house,
  Twenty men their arms did carry,
And he has stow'n this lady fair,
  On purpose her to marry.

III.

And when he cam, he surrounded the house,
  No tidings there cam before him,
Or else the lady would have been gone,
  For still she did abhor him.

IV.

Wi' murnfu' cries, and wat'ry eyes,
  Fast hauding by her mother,
Wi' murnfu' cries, and wat'ry eyes,
  They were parted frae each other.

V.

Nae time he gied her to be dress'd,
  As ladies do when they're bride O !
But he hastened and hurried her awa',
  And he row'd her in his plaid O !

VI.

They rade till they cam to Ballyshine,
  At Ballyshine they tarried ;
He bought to her a cotton gown,
  Yet ne'er would she be married.

VII.

Three held her up before the priest,
  Four carried her to bed O !
Wi' wat'ry eyes, and murnfu' sighs,
  When she behind was laid O !

*   *   *   *   *

VIII.

" O be content, be content,
  " Be content to stay, lady,
" For you are my wedded wife,
  " Unto my dying day, lady !"

CHORUS.

" Be content, be content,

   " Be content to stay, lady,

" For you are my wedded wife,

   " Unto my dying day, lady !

IX.

" My father is Rob Roy called,

   " M'Gregor is his name, lady,

" In all the county where he dwells,

   " He does succeed the fame, lady !

     " Be content, &c.

X.

" My father he has cows and ewes,

   " And goats he has eneuch, lady,

" And you and twenty thousand merks,

   " Will make me a man complete, lady ! *

     " Be content," &c.

---

* For an account of the circumstances founded
on in the Ballad, vide Criminal Trials illustrative
of Rob Roy, p. 14-22.—This singular individual's
son, James, was the father of Gregor, who drop-
ped the name of Campbell, and assumed that of
Drummond.—He was a butcher by trade, and
left a daughter, who married one Brown, a per-
fumer, who having been killed by the carelessness
of the driver of a stage coach, his widow and child-

Paul Jones.

The following is taken from Mr. Pitcairn's MS. Collection of Ballads, &c.—It was written down by him from the recitation of an Old Lady, who gave the Song the name of PAUL JONES, on which account it is so termed here.—Mr. P. remarks, that it "was much sung in Edinburgh by the populace, on occasion of Paul Jones making his appearance in the Firth of Forth; and also during the strenuous opposition in Scotland, and the consequent riots which took place, during the discussion of the Popish Bill. It was afterwards revived during the threatened invasion of Britain by Bonaparte, in ridicule of the attempt; but I have not hitherto been able to procure either a MS. or printed set of this curious Song.—This Ballad is sung to the now popular air of ' Were a' noddin'.' "

ren brought an action of damages against the proprietors, in which they were successful, and obtained exemplary damages.——For this *valuable* piece of genealogical information, the Editor is indebted to Alexander Campbell, Esq.

I.

" O dear, Marg'et, are ye within ?

 " When I heard the news, I but to rin,

" Down the gate to tell ye,

 " Down the gate to tell ye,

 " Down the gate to tell ye,

" We'll no be left our skin !

II.

" O dear, woman ! O dear ! O dear !

 " There ne'er was the like o' this since Marr's year,

" And I'm a' pantin',

 " Pantin' pantin',

 " I'm a pantin',

" Frae my heart here !

III.

" Weel kent I, that a' was nae right,

 " For I dream'd o' red and green, a' last night,

" And three cats fighting,

 " And three cats fighting,

 " And three cats fighting,

" I waukened wi' the fright !

IV.

" But fare ye weel, woman, for I maun gae rin,

 " Do you ken if your neighbour Elspet be in ?

" And auld Rob the barber,

 " And auld Rob the barber,

 " And auld Rob the barber,

" For I maun tell him !"

V.

" Stay a wee woman, an' tell us a' out,

 " They're bringing in Popery, I doubt, an' I doubt,

" And a sad reformation,

 " And a sad reformation,

 " And a sad reformation,

" In a' the kirks about!

VI.

" Little do we see, but meickle do we hear,

 " The French and Americans are a' comin' here,

" An' we'll a' be murdered,

 " An' we'll a' be murdered,

 " An' we'll a' be murdered,

" Before the New-Year!"

VII.

"Whish't woman, whish't! I thought I heard a gun."

 "Hout na' Marg'et!—it's me, I'm fash'd wi' win'.

" An' I'm glad when it wins awa'.

 " An' I'm glad when it wins awa',

 " An' I'm glad when it wins awa',

" Free frae behin'!

VIII.

" But never ye fear woman—let them a' come,

 "For I'll wield my rock yet, for a' their necks' horn,

" Before that I yield it,

 " Before that I yield it,

 " Before that I yield it,

" To ony Frenchman born.

IX.

" For dinna ye mind, on this very floor,

 " How we a reek'd out, an' a' to Shirramuir,

" Wi' stanes in our aprons,

 " Wi' stanes in our aprons,

 " Wi' stanes in our aprons,

" And wrought skaith I'm sure ?"

The Jolly Hawk and the Tearsel.

The ensuing Song is the production of the amiable Lord Binning ; of whom several very interesting particulars will be found, in the recently publish- ed Memoirs of Lady Murray. —A Brief Sketch of his Life is given in Walpole's Royal and Noble Authors, vol. V. p. 142. Park's Edition.

I.

I had a jolly hawk, and a tearsel of my own.

 Fal, &c.

Come from as good an airy, as ever yet was known.

 Fal, &c.

He was but newly enter'd, when that it came to pass,

He fell in love with a solan goose, and flew into the

 Bass,

  Fal, &c.

II.

When he arrived there, the goose to him did say,

I pray, good master tearsel, what brought you here
    away ?

To which the tearsel answer'd, I'm come to get an egg

With you, sweet mistress goose, if you'll please to lift
    your leg.

III.

The jealous solan gander put on an angry face,

I pray, good master tearsel, I redd you leave this
    place,

If you don't do it quickly, your stay you shall repent,

Wou'd you spoil our brood of solan geese, and vex the
    President ? *

IV.

To which the tearsel answer'd, I dinna care a f——t,

Gin ye winna len' me your wife, I'll ha'd me wi' a
    scart ;

Ye may keep her to ye're sel', but ye needna look sae
    fierce,

For I'll kiss and clap my scart, and ye may kiss my
    a——se !

V.

Ye're seamaws and tamie nories, into my bed I'll take,

Nor will I spare a marrot, nor yet a kitty-weake,

Neither goose nor sandy lavrock, nor whaup shall e'er
    gae free,

But ev'ry bird into the Bass, shall lay an egg to me !

---

* President Dalrymple of North Berwick.

VI.

The solan goose offended, to hear him crack sae crouse,

Says ye're a cursed liar, Sir, as I'm a solan goose ;

For if you do but touch a bird, be she either wife or
lass.

Ye shall hae cause to rue the day, that e'er ye saw
the Bass !

VII.

O Sir, ye'er but a stanchel, or else a ring-tail'd kite,

Then turning round his rumple, he iu his face did
sh—te ;

The hawk in doleful dolor, did wipe his sh—en e'e,

And was content to take his wing, and waft him o'er
the sea.

VIII.

He lighted on Tam Tallen, and pearch'd upon a tow'r,

A pox confound the solan goose, the husband of the
whore,

For he's blindit a' my eye, and he's claggit a' my
wing,

And the d—l confound his rotten doup, his sh—te it
stinks o' ling !

IX.

Mean-while the dolefu' master, was in a deep despair,

A capias gae to Nicoly, see what's become o' Blair,

Gae send out little Stev'nson, and see that he be sure

To call out Grova Nicoly, to waft about the lure.

X.

What ail'd the careless rascal to hound him down the
  wind,

I'll loose my harvest hawking, unless my hawk I find;

Quoth Haddington I'm sorry, quoth Binny I could
  greet;

Quoth Tam, my Lord, I'll seek your hawk upon my
  barefoot feet.

XI.

But in came William Bower, with pleasure in his face,

My Lord ye're hawk's came back,—but he's in a sh—ten
  case!

My Lord was all in rapture to hear the gladsome tale,

Tak that to buy ye brandy, and that to buy ye ale!

XII.

How fickle and uncertain are all our earthly joys,

When the losing of a hawk, all our harvest hope de-
  stroys:

But we'll thraw about each hawk's neck, and hang
  each yelping hound,

And tak ourselves to tippenny, where joys alone
  abound!

O what a Parish.

TUNE—" Bonny Dundee."

The Editor has not, until very recently, been able
to procure any more than the first stanza, or rather the *Chorus*, of this extremely spirited production.   He is ignorant of the circumstances
which gave rise to the Song, no popular tradition
on the subject having hitherto reached him.

CHORUS.

O what a parish, what a terrible parish !
O what a parish is that o' Dunkell !
They hae hangit the minister, drown't the precentor,
Dang dawn the steeple, an' druken the bell !

I.

Tho' the steeple was down, the kirk was still stannin',
They biggit a lum* whare the bell used to hang,
A stell-pat they gat, and they brew'd Highland whisky,
On Sundays they drank it, an' ranted an' sang !
    O what a Parish, &c.

* Chimney.

II.

O ! had you but seen how gracefu' it luikit,
To see the crammed pews so socially join ;
Macdonald the piper stuck up in the pu'pit,
He made the pipes skirle sweet music divine.

    O ! what a Parish, &c.

III.

When the heart cheering spirit had mounted the gar-
    rėt,
To a ball on the green, they a' did adjourn,
Maids wi' their coats kiltit, they skippit and liltit,
When tired, they shook hands, and a' hame did return.

    O ! what a Parish, &c.

IV.

Wad the kirks in our Britain, haud sic social meetings,
Nae warnin' they'd need frae a tinklin' bell,
For true love and friendship, wad ca' them thegither,
Far better than roarin' o' horrors o' hell.

    O ! what a Parish, &c.

My Wife shall hae her Will.

To be sung to its own particular Tune.

The Editor is indebted to Mr. Pitcairn's MS. Collection for this Song. He states, that "it was "taken from the recitation of Miss K—, an Old "Lady, who mentions it as having been popular "when she was a girl, (about half a century ago,) "but she did not recollect of ever seeing it in any written or printed Collection."

I.

If my dear wife should chance to gang
   Wi' me to Edinburgh town,
Into a shop I will her tak,
   And buy her a new gown.

But if my dear wife should hain the charge,
   As I expect she will,
And if she says "the auld ane will do,"
   By my word she shall hae her will !

II.

If my dear wife should wish to gang,
   To see a neighbour or a friend.
A horse or a chaise I will provide,
   And a servant to attend;

But if my dear wife shall hain the charge,
   As I expect she will;
And if she says, she " will walk on foot,"
   By my word she shall hae her will.

III.

If my dear wife shall bring me a son,
   As I expect she will;
Cake and wine I will provide,
   And a nurse to nurse the child.

But if my dear wife shall hain the charge,
   As I expect she will,
And if she says, she'll nurse it hersell,
   By my word she shall hae her will.

Finis.

THE

BALLAD BOOK.

MUSSEL MOU'D CHARLIE.

EDINBURGH:
MDCCCXXVII.

CHARLES LESLY (better known by the name of "*Mussel mou'd Charlie*," from a singular protusion of his nether lip, in the form of a muscle—and whose portraiture adorns our title-page,) was, for the greater part of last century, a celebrated peripatetick Ballad-singer in the Town and County of Aberdeen.

Of his early years, nothing authentic can be discovered; though Traditionknows him only as an itinerant ballad-singer from his youth. Fame, however, speaks of him as a rank and irreclaimable Jacobite, having been OUT in the rebellions of "*Fifteen*," and "*Forty-five*;" and as having not only aided the *great cause* with his *sword*, but likewise employed his *pen* in its favour. He is said to have been the author of sundry Jacobite compositions, and especially of that severe phillippic on *the Duke*, commencing, "Will ye go to Crookieden." These songs not only cheered and animated his fellow soldiers during the fatigues of their arduous enterprises in the days of yore, but were also, in later times, the chief sources of their Author's livelihood: for, somewhat Homer-like, did the venerable Charles Lesly sing his own compositions through the streets of Aberdeen, for his daily subsistence; and it is not to be doubted that he ever wanted a share of that *gueed awmous* for which the place is remarkable, although we do not hear that upon his death there was any competition for the honour of his birth-place among the *cities* of Aberdeenshire.

As Charles advanced in years, he made the town of Aberdeen his most permanent residence, and there maintained, to the last, the field of ballad-singing against an host of more youthful competitors, who attempted, by the promulgation of modern and more refined ditties, to depose poor Charlie from the enviable monopoly which he had so long enjoyed. Fortunately, however, for this ancient hero of rhyme, the more sober citizens, who had so long listened with pleasure to his "deep and hollow roar," and admired the eccentricity of his person and habits, began to vindicate his rights, as being founded on a clear *prescriptive title*, he having "danced and sung," according to the biographical poem annexed, no less a period than one hundred and five years! Indeed, to lose Charlie, would have been depriving Aberdeen of a singular portion of living antiquity, that had become quite identified with the Town and its inhabitants. The consequence was, that Charlie's rivals were put to the rout, and himself allowed to rest in his ancient monopoly unmolested.

Death at last " closed the mussel-mou" of Charlie Lesly, who departed this life at Old Raine, his native place, in the year 1792, at the extraordinary age of 105. This sorrowful event was announced to the world, by the following paragraph in the North British Weekly Magazine for the month of October, 1792 : " Died lately at Oldrain, in Aberdeenshire, aged 105, Charles Lesly, a hawker, or ballad-singer, well known in that country by the name of *Mussel mou'd Charlie.* He followed his occupation till within a few weeks of his death."

Like other public characters whose demise gives occasion to many political intrigues and bickerings, Charles Lesly had scarcely breathed his last till numerous brethren of the craft flocked to the metropolis of the shire, ambitious of acquiring the office which he had so long and so honourably maintained. The office, however, seems, from the want of a competent successor, to have been put in commission; for we find, in the twenty-third verse of the annexed ballad, that "Blind Jamie," and "Ross" were appointed to deliver out the *mussel mou'd* relics to the inconsolable Aberdonians.

With respect to the political creed of the subject of this memoir, we can hardly, after all, think him such a determined Jacobite as has been represented. For although his before mentioned phillippic against the commander of the Royal army in " the forty-five," is well enough for a rank Jacobite, yet it cannot be denied that *Prince Charlie* himself comes in for a pretty severe rub on the occasion, as well as the Duke; which shows that our Author was a good deal of an humourist:

> Will ye go to Crookieden,
>   Bonny laddie, Highland laddie,
> There you'll see Charlie and his men,
>   My bonnie Highland laddie.
>
> All the whigs will gang to hell,
>   Bonnie laddie, Highland laddie,
> CHARLIE *he'll be there himsell,*
>   My bonny Highland laddie.
>
> Satan sits in the black nook,
>   A bonnie laddie, Highland laddie,
> Riving sticks to roast the Duke,
>   My bonnie Highland laddie.

Notwithstanding the public avocations of Mr. Lesly, and the many hazards and hardships he must have suffered during so long a life, he seems to have been not insensible to the more social duties of the married state. For we find, in the outset of one of his ballads, the following notice of his *purchase* of a Wife in Edinburgh :

> " I bought a wife in Edinbrugh
> For a bawbee ;—
> I got a farthing in again,
> To buy tobacco wi."—

Whether any rise in the price of wives in this Scottish Smithfield has taken place since the days of Mrs. Lesly, we do not know ; only this we know, that there is a considerable advance in the article of *tocher* : for all that mussel mou'd Charlie received by his matrimonial *bargain* was, according to his poetical biographer, the sum and quantity of — " a farthing's worth of cut tobacco !!" *—*Eheu ! quam tempora mutantur !—*

In a collection of *Penny Ballads*, *penes* Mr. Maidment, there is one entitled, " A new song, called the Jacobite's Lamentation;–Composed and sold by Charles Lesly, Flying Stationer, the Poet." It is printed along with "The True Britain's Thought," and "Johnnie

---

* Being one half of the price, which was returned by way of *luck-penny*.

Armstrong's last good night ;" and bears the imprint,
" Edinburgh, Printed for Charles Lesly, Flying Stationer, the Author, 1746." If it were not the case that the
orthodox Jacobite tenets of mussel-mou'd Charlie were
abundantly conspicuous from other sources, this " Jacobite's Lamentation," which is a violent tirade against
his favourite doctrines, and party, would stagger our
belief. We are, therefore, inclined to attribute it solely
to the roguery of some wag, in order to torment poor
Charlie, whose faith burned with almost insane fervour
for the opposite party.

Considering his popular fame as a poet and ballad-
singer, the steadiness of his political principles, and his
extreme old age, we may safely aver in the words of the
following ditty, composed on the occasion of his death,
that " few men like him are now alive."

" SIC TRANSIT GLORIA MUNDI !"

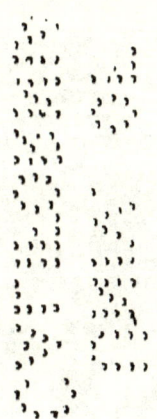

CHARLIE LESLIE of ABERDEENSHIRE, who died 1782 Aged 105.

MUSSEL MOU'D CHARLIE.

AIR—" *Highland Laddie.*"

O dolefu' rings the bell o' Raine !
  Bonny Laddie, Highland Laddie,
For Charlie ne'er will sing again,
  My bonnie Highland laddle.

Grim death has clos'd his mussel mou',
  Bonny Laddie, Highland Laddie,
Be this a warning bell to you,
  My bonnie Highland Laddie.

He's dead, and shortly will be rotten,
  Bonnie Laddie, Highland Laddie,
But he must never be forgotten,
  My bonnie Highland Laddie.

He danc'd and sang years five score and five,
  Bonnie Laddie, Highland Laddie,
Few men like him are now alive,
  My bonnie Highland Laddie.

Gae lads and lasses to the fair,
  Bonnie Laddie, Highland Laddie,
For Charlie ne'er will meet you there,
  My bonnie Highland Laddie.

Nor in the streets of Aberdeen,
  Bonnie Laddie, Highland Laddie,
Will his lang spindle shanks be seen,
  My bonny Highland Laddie.

The hardest heart would surely melt,
  Bonnie Laddie, Highland Laddie,
To see his wig, hat, coat, and belt,
  My bonny Highland Laddie.

To see them by a broomstick borne,
  Bonny Laddie, Highland Laddie,
To scare the rooks frae early corn,
  My bonny Highland Laddie.

His bag where ballad books have been,
  Bonny Laddie, Highland Laddie,
In rags hang wagging on a pin,
  My bonny Highland Laddie.

And his lang staff, which lang he wore
   Bonny Laddie, Highland Laddie.
Drive off the dogs frae the kirk door.
   My bonny Highland Laddie.

Had I the powers of Parson Wesley,
   Bonny Laddie, Highland Laddie,
I'd preach in praise of Charlie Lesly,
   My bonny Highland Laddie.

For, troth, he was a canty carle, and
   Bonny Laddy, Highland Laddie,
Many a brave ballad made, and garland,
   My bonny Highland Laddie.

And all his garlands, all his ballads,
   Bonny Laddie, Highland Laddie,
All bonny lasses pleased, and all lads,
   My bonny Highland Laddie.

The fame of Charlie wander'd far,
   Bonny Laddie, Highland Laddie,
Through Angus, Buchan, Mearns, and Mar,
   My bonny Highland Laddie.

Strathbogie can, and Garioch, tell,
   Bonny Laddie, Highland Laddie,
That oft he sent the Whigs to hell,
   My bonny Highland Laddie.

And how he went to Crookieden,
  Bonny Laddie, Highland Laddie,
To see Prince Charlie's Highlandmen,
  My Bonny Highland Laddie.

And how, for comfort of his life,
  Bonnie Laddie, Highland Laddie,
In Edinbrugh he bought a wife,
  My bonny Highland Laddie.

Each Ballad a bawbee him brought,
  Bonny Laddie, Highland Laddie,
And for that sum his wife he bought,
  My bonny Highland Laddie.

Her tocher was not quite worth a plack O,
  Bonny Laddie, Highland Laddie,
A farthing's worth of cut tobacco,
  My bonny Highland Laddie.

The songs he sang, and many more,
  Bonnie Laddie, Highland Laddie.
And deep and hollow was his roar,
  My bonny Highland Laddie.

Those songs in the lang nights of winter,
  Bonny Laddie, Highland Laddie,
He made, and Chalmers* was the printer,
  My bonny Highland Laddie.

      * A Printer in Aberdeen.

O mourn, good master Chalmers, mourn,
  Bonnie Laddie, Highland Laddie,
For Charlie will no more return,
  My bonny Highland Laddie.

Blind Jamie now, and Ross, they say,
  Bonny Laddie, Highland Laddie,
Maun sing your books when he's away,
  My bonny Highland Laddie.

And so farewell, good people all,
  Bonny Laddie, Highland Laddie,
Both old and young, both great and small,
  My bonny Highland Laddie.

Good luck betide you, late and early,
  Bonny Laddie, Highland Laddie,
And may you live as long as Charlie,
  My bonny Highland Laddie.

THE WIDOW O' WESTMORELAND.

~ ~~~ ~~~~~ ~~~~

There was a widow in Westmoreland,
  And she never had a child but ane ;
And she prayed, aye, baith nicht and day,
  She micht keep her maidenhead lang.

" O haud your tongue, my mither dear,
  And say na mair to me,
For a jolly young man o' the king's life-guard,
  My maidenhead's tane frae me."

" Awa, awa, ye ill woman,
  Some ill death mat ye dee !
If a jolly young man o' the king's life-guard,
  Your maidenhead's tane frae thee."

But she is on to her true-love gane,
    As fast as gang cou'd she ;
Says, " Gie me back my maidenhead,
    For my mammy sair dings me."

He's buskit her, and he's deckit her,
    And he's laid her on his bed ;
He laid her head whare her feet was afore,
    Gied her back her maidenhead.

He buskit her, and he deckit her,
    Wi' a rose in ilka han' ;
And bade her come to Saint Mary's kirk,
    To see his rich weddan.

Now she is on to her mither gane,
    As fast as gang cou'd she ;
Says, " I'm as leal a maiden, mither dear,
    As that night ye bore me."

He buskit me, and he deckit me,
    And he laid me on his bed ;
He laid my head whare my feet war afore,
    Gied me back my maidenhead.

He buskit me, and he deckit me,
   Wi' a rose in ilka han' ;
Syne bade me come to Saint Mary's kirk,
   To see his rich weddan."

" O never on fit," her mither said,
   " But on hie horse ye sal ride ;
And four-and-twenty gay ladies
   Sal a' walk by your side."

" O wha is this," the bride she cried,
   " That comes sae hie to me ?
Is this the Widow's dochter o' Westmoreland
   Wha gaed hame and told her mammie ?

How could she do't, how did she do't,
   How could she do't ?—for shame !
Eleven lang nichts I lay wi' a man,
   But never told that to ane."

" If eleven lang nichts ye've lain wi' a man,
   My bed-fellow ye'se never be ;
I'll tak the Widow's dochter o' Westmoreland
   Wha gaed hame and told her mammie."

II.

THE SLEEPY MERCHANT.

an "Aiken Drum"

There cam a merchant to this toun,
I wat he was a clever loon,
And at the door as he stood boun,
  He chappit and cam in :
    He called for a bonnie lass,
    He called for a bonnie lass,
    He called for a bonnie lass,
  He cou'dna lie his leen.

The merchant's bed it was weel made,
And the merchant lad in it was laid,
A dram for him she did provide,
  Bade him drink and lie down ;
    For ye are the sleepy merchant,
    For ye are the sleepy merchant,
    For ye are the sleepy merchant,
  That canna lie your leen.

And whan the sun it was weel up,
The lassie startit to her feet,—
" I am as leal a maiden yet,
    As I lay doun yestreen :
        For ye're but a sleepy merchant,
        For ye're but a sleepy merchant,
        For ye're but a sleepy merchant,
    That canna lie your leen.

And whan the breakfast it was by,
Fareweel to her, was a' he could say,
Fareweel to her, was a' he could say,
    But I will come again :
        For he was a sleepy merchant,
        For he was a sleepy merchant,
        For he was a sleepy merchant,
    That cou'dna lie his leen.

And whan the market it was oure,
To that same house he did repair,
And at the door as he stood there,
    He chappit and cam in :
        He called for the bonnie lassie
        He called for the bonnie lassie
        He called for the bonnie lassie
    That lay wi' him yestreen.

The merchant's bed it was weel made,
And the merchant lad in it was laid,
A dram for him she did provide,
  Bade him drink and lie down :
    " For ye're but a sleepy merchant,
    For ye're but a sleepy merchant,
    For ye're but a sleepy merchant,
  Ye canna lie your leen."

Atween the bowster and the wa',
I wat he quickly toom'd it a',
I wat he quickly toom'd it a',
  And syne sat up and sang :
    " Come to your bed my bonnie lass,
    Come to your bed, my bonnie lass,
    Come to your bed my bonnie lass,
  I canna lie my leen."

And lang afore the brak o' day,
Richt kindly to him she did say,
Richt kindly to him she did say,
  " Pray, tell to me your name ?"
    " Ca' me the sleepy merchant,
    Ca' me the sleepy merchant,
    Ca' me the sleepy merchant,
  That canna lie my leen.

But fesh* ye ben the cradle plaid,
And I'll gie ye a braw new faik,†.
Be sure ye dinna let them see't,
   Till I gae frae the toun :
      For they'll mock ye wi' the merchaut,
      For they'll mock ye wi' the merchant,
      For they'll mock ye wi' the merchant,
   That ye lay wi' yestreen."

And whan the breakfast it was bye,
Unto her comrades she did say,—
" Braw news I hae to tell the day,
   Sin the merchant's gane frae toun :
      For I hae got a braw new faik,
      And frae my merry merchant lad,
      And frae my merry merchant lad,
   That I lay wi' yestreen."

But whan she gaed but to fesh it ben,
Behaud what follow'd after then,
There was naithing but the cradle plaid,
   Wi' the tows that tied the same :

---

* *Fesh*—fetch.

† *Faik*—a checked plaid usually worn by Shepherds.

" Foul fa' ye for a merchant,
 Ye're but a cheating merchant,
 Ye're but a cheating merchant,
Ye micht hae lain your leen."

Whan twenty weeks war come and gane,
This merchant he came back again,
And at the door as he stood boun,
 He thus begoud and sang :—
  " Mind ye upo' the merchant,
  Mind ye upo' the merchant,
  Mind ye upo' the merchant,
 That cou'dna lie his leen ?"

The lassie she sat at her wheel,
The tears cam trickling to her heel ;
Then up and to the door she ran—
 " Ha ! ha ! he's come again !
  Here comes my merry merchant,
  Here comes my merry merchant,
  Here comes my merry merchant lad,
 That wadna lie his leen."

" O my dear, how may this be,
That ye're sae blue aneath the ee,
That ye're sae blae aneath the ee ?
 Ye hae na lain your leen.

Why did ye mock the merchant,
Why did ye mock the merchant,
Why did ye mock the merchant,
Ye bear his pack in your wame !

He's tane the lassie by the hand,
And tied her up in wedlock band,
And now she is the merchant's wife,
And she lives in Aberdeen :
For she's married wi' the merchant,
She's married wi' the merchant,
She's married wi' the merchant lad,
And he needna lie his leen.

NOTE

THE SLEEPY MERCHANT.

That ye're sae blae aneath the ee,
Ye hae na lain your leen.—v. 14.

It is considered among the vulgar a sure sign of the unchastity of a young woman to have the under eyelid of a blackish or dark blue colour. Tytler, in " The bonnie brucket lassie," takes notice of this characteristic :

The bonnie brucket lassie,
She's blue beneath the een.

And in the old song of " The shearing is no for you," we observe the proverbial expression

Your blue below the ee,
Whar a maiden shouldna be.

Physicians, however, do not recognize this as a mark of unchastity ; but all the *howdies* declare that it is a *breeding* sign.   " If under the lower eyelid the veins be swelled and appear clearly and the eyes be something discoloured, it is a certain sign she is with child, unless &c.—*Aristotle's Masterpiece.*   *Green* was also a sign of conception :—

> " Four and twenty belted knights
>   Were playing at the chess;
> Whan out and came her, fair Janet,
>   As green as ony gress."
>
> *Young Tamlane.*

III.

THE MAGDALENE'S LAMENT.

And she, poor jade, withoutten din,
Is sent to Leith-wynd fit* to spin,
Wi' heavy heart, and claithing thin,
    And hungry wame,
And ilka month a well paid skin
    To mak her tame.

Ramsay.

As I cam in by Tanzie's wood,
And in by Tanzie's mill,
Four-and-twenty o' Geordie's men
Kiss'd me against my will.
    Diddle dow, &c. &c.

---

* The house of correction formerly at the foot of Leith-wynd, Edinburgh.

For ance I was a lady fair,
   And lik'd the young men well,
But now I'm in the correction-house,
   A woful tale to tell!

Whan we were in yon tavern-house,
   We liv'd in a good case,
We neither wanted meat nor drink,
   Nor bonnie lads to kiss.

But now I'm in the correction-house,
   And sair, sair do I mourn;
But now I'm in the correction-house,
   And whipped to my turn.

A wee drap cabbage-kail in a cog,
   A cog and a wee drap burn;
A wee drap cabbage-kail in a cog,
   And a bodle bap aboon.

But if I were at libertie,
   As I hope to be soon,
I hope to be a married wife
   Whan a'thir days are done.

Awa wi' your slavery hiremen,
  Sic lads as ye ca' foremen,
They rise by the cock, and claw the kail-pat,
  And that's the knacks o' your hiremen,

Awa wi' your mealy miller,
  Awa wi' your mealy miller,
He's married a wife, and he's brocht her hame,
  And canna do nathing till her.

Awa wi' your limey mason,
  Awa wi' your limey mason,
He's married a wife, and he's brocht her hame,
  And he's ne'er put her gown frae lacing.

Awa wi' your blackie sutor,
  Awa wi' your blackie sutor,
He's married a wife, and he's brocht her hame,
  And he's flung the black about her.

But I'm for the ranting gardener,
  But I'm for the ranting gardener,
He pu'd me a flower on Michaelmas day,
  And it's sair'd me aye sin fernyear.

JOCK SHEEP

Is evidently the Scottish version of the English ballad of
" The Baffled Knight, or Lady's Policy," published in
Percy's Reliques, which is " given with some corrections
from a manuscript copy, and collated with two printed
ones in the Roman character in the Pepys collection."
The English copy is decidedly inferior in point of
humour and fancy.

JOCK SHEEP

———

THERE was a knight and a lady bright
  Set a true tryst to the broom;
The tane to meet at twal o'clock,
  The tither true at noon.

Whan they cam to the gude greenwud,
  He lichtly laid her doun;—
" O spare me now, kind Sir, " she says,
  " For spoiling o' my goun.

Do ye na see my father's castle?
  It's guarded weel about,
And ye sall hae your wills o' me,
  Therein, and no thairout."

But whan she cam to her father's yett
  Sae lichtly she lap doun ;
She's shut the door, behind her,
  Says, " Whistle o' your thumb !

And whistle o' your thumb, Jock Sheep,
  And whistle o' your thumb ;
Sae stand you there, Jock Sheep," she says,
  " And whistle o' your thumb.

You're like a cock my father has,
  He wears the double kaim,
He claps his wings but craws nane,
  And I think ye are like him.
            And whistle, &c.

You're like a flower in my father's garden,
  They ca't the marigold ;
And he that wadna whan he could,
  He shanna when he wold.
            And whistle, &c.

You're like a steed my father has,
  He's tethered on yon loan ;
He hangs his head out o'er the mare,
  But darena venture on."
            And whistle, &c.

He's turned him right and round about,
    And swore he'd got the scorn ;
But he's to hae his wills o' her,
    On Monday or the morn.

He's tane a mantle him about,
    Wi' a cod* upon his wame ;
And he's on to gude greenwud,
    Like a lady in travelling.

Then word's cum to her father's castle,
    And thro' the ha' its gane,
That there was a lady in gude greenwud
    And she was a-travelling.

She's tane her mantle her about,
    Her key's out oure her arm ;
And she is gane to gude greenwud
    To see this lady wi' bairn.

But whan she cam to gude greenwud,
    She saw nae lady there,
But a knicht upon a milk-white steed
    Kaiming down his yellow hair.

---

* *Cod*—pillow.

" Ye're welcome here, my dear," he says,
  " Ye're welcome here, my dow;
Sin ye'er sae trusty to your tryst,
  My dear ye sanna rue."

He's tane her by the milk-white hand,
  Sae lichtly laid her doun,
And whan he loot her up again,
  Says, " Whistle o' your thumb :

And whistle o' your thumb, fair may,
  And whistle o' your thumb ;
Sae stand ye there, fair may," he says,
  " And whistle o' your thumb.

Ye said I was like your father's cock,
 . He wore the double kame ;
He clapt his wings but craw'd nane ;
  And ye thoucht I was like him.
         And whistle, &c.

Ye said I was like a flow'r in your father's garden,
  They ca't the marigold :
And he that wadna whan he could,
  He shanna whan he wold.
         And whistle, &c.

Ye said I was like your father's steed,
    Was tether'd on yon loan :
He hung his head out oure the mare,
    But I think he's ventur'd on !"
               Sae whistle, &c.

" O had I staid in my father's castle,
    And sew'd the silken seam !
But sin you've tane your wills o' me,
    You may conduct me hame."

He's set her on his milk-white steed,
    And took her to the ha' ;
Nae lord or lady look'd sae blythe,
    As them twa 'mang them a'.

EPITAPH ON JOCK SHEEP.

Hic conditur Joannes Ovis,
Who, in love matters, was no novice ;
Puellam validè compressit,
As ancient ditty doth express it.

———

The above Epitaph was written by a friend, who, on reading the ballad thought it worthy of such an accompaniment.

VI.

The lassie and the laddie
  Gaed out to wauk the mill,
And waly was the weel made bed
  The laddie lay intil.

The laddie gaed to bar the door,
  The lassie gaed wi' him,
And ae it cam into her mind,
  Wi' him she wad lie doun.

She's casten aff her petticoat,
  And sae has she her goun,
Atween the laddie and the wa',
  I wat she did lie doun.

Up gat the nakit fallow,
  And ran frae toun to toun,
And there he spied his master,
  Was walking up and doun.

" The cauld's tane me, master,
  The cauld has taken me,
The hire-quean has tane my bed,
  And I am forc'd to flee.·

O I hae serv'd ye seven lang years,
  And never sought a fee,
And I will serve ye ither seven,
  And haud that quean frae me.

It's up the loan o' Charltoun,
  And doun the water o' Dee,
And oure the Cairn-o'-mount, master,
  And farder I could flee."

VII.

THE FRIAR.

———

Can this be one of the squibs, so liberally fulminated
at the Roman Catholic Priests and Friars, during
the days of Sir David Lindsay; when they were saty-
rized as paying more devotion to " marit wyfis " and
" lustie maydens," than to their book and psalter? See
an English copy of this Ballad in *Durfey's Pills to
purge Melancholy*, vol. I., p. 34, under the title of
" The Fryer and the Maid."

———

O listen, and I will ye tell,
    Wi' a falaldirry, falaldirry,
How a Friar in love wi' a lassie fell,
    Wi' a falee and leetee and a lee,
        tiddle, tiddle, tee.

The Friar cam to the maiden's bed-side,
  Wi' a fal. &c.
And asked for her maidenhead,
  Wi' a falee, &c.

"O I wad grant you your desire,
  Wi' a fal. &c.
If it was na for fear o' hell's burning fire,"
  Wi' a falee, &c.

"O' hell's burning fire ye need have na doubt,
  Wi' a fal. &c.
Altho' ye were in I could sing ye out,"
  Wi' a falee, &c.

"O an I grant to you this thing,
  Wi' a fal. &c.
Some money ye unto me maun bring,"
  Wi' a falee, &c.

He brocht her the money and did it down tell ;
  Wi' a fal. &c.
She had a white claith spread oure the well,
  Wi' a falee, &c.

The lassie cries, " my master does come,"
      Wi' a Fal. &c.
The Friar cries " Whar sall 1 run ?"
      Wi' a falee, &c.

" O ye'll dow ye in below this claith,
      Wi' a fal. &c.
That ye be seen I wad be laith,"
      Wi' a falee, &c.*

The Friar cries, " I'm in the well,"
      Wi' a fal. &c.
" I care na though ye war in hell,
      Wi' a falee, &c.*

---

* *Var.*—O ye will go behind yon screen,
      Wi' a fal, &c.
    There by my master ye winna be seen,
      Wi' a falee, &c.

    Then in behind the screen she him sent,
      Wi' a fal, &c.
    And he fell into the well by accident,
      Wi' a falee, &c.

Then the Friar cried, with piteous moan,
Wi' a fal. &c.
O! help! O help! or else I am gone,"
Wi' a falee, &c.

" Ye said ye wad sing me out o' hell,
Wi' a fal. &c.
Sing yoursel out o' the well,"
Wi' a falee, &c.

" If ye'll help me out I will be gone,
Wi' a fal. &c.
Back to you I'll never come,"
Wi' a falee, &c.

She helpit him out, and bade him begone ;
Wi' a fal. &c.
But the Friar asked his money again,
Wi' a falee. &c.

" For your money there's na much matter,
Wi' a fal. &c.
To mak you pay for fumbling* our water,"
Wi' a falee, &c.

---

* Qu. *Drumbling*—i. e. troubling or mudying.

The Friar he gaed up the street,
     Wi' a fal. &c.
Hanging his lugs like a new washen sheet, ·
     Wi' a falee, &c.

Then a' wha heard it commend this fair maid,
     Wi' a fal. &c.
For the nimble trick to the Friar she play'd.
     Wi' a falee, &c.

———

* * *

The beef, and the bacon,
 The capon and the hare,
And a' kin kind o' kitchen,
 Was weel provided there.

In cam Lizzie Ogilvie,
 Wi' her silk-and-worsted goun,—
" Sit about, brave maidens,
 And gie to me some room;

For there's ten ell in my petticoat,
 And nine into my goun:
Sae sit about, brave maidens,
 And gie to me some room."

* * *

EARL OF ERROL.

Gilbert Hay, tenth Earl of Errol, the hero of this singular production, was married at Kinnaird, 7th January, 1658, to Lady Catherine Carnegy, youngest daughter of James, second Earl of Southesk. The tradition of the country is that the lady actually sued her husband for a divorce on the ground of impotency, and that the incidents really took place as detailed in the ballad, but I have been unable to discover the truth of this tradition. The following excerpt, however, from a note on a South country version of this ballad, preserved in Mr. Sharpe's " Ballad Book," bears strong evidence of the truth of the tradition. It is contained in a letter from Keith of Benholm to Captain Brown at Paris, which, after mentioning other news of the day, concludes :—" Lastly, the sadd (and not lyke heard of in this land amongst eminent persons,) story of the Erll of Errol's impotencie, which is lyke, being cum to public hearing, to draw deeper betuix him and Southesk, than is alledgit it hath done 'twixt him and Southesk's daughter. These are the meane emergents we are taken up with, whilst beyond sea empyres are overturning."—*Scoone, 22d Feb.* 1659.

EARL OF ERROL.

O Errol is a bonnie place,*
   Into the simmer time ;
The apples they grow red and white,
   And the pears they grow green.

   And the ranting o't, and the danting o't,
      According as ye ken ;
   And the thing we ca' the danting o't,
      Is—Errol's na a man !

---

* Errol is situated in the Carse of Gowrie ; a district famed
for the excellence of its fruit.

O Errol's place is a bonnie place,
  It stands upo' yon plain ;
But what's the use o' Errol's place ?
  He's na like ither men.

" As I cam in by yon canal,
  And by yon bowling green,
I micht hae pleas'd the best Carnegie,
  That ever bore the name.

Tho' your name be Dame Cathrine Carnegie,
  And mine Sir Gilbert Hay,
I'll gar your father sell Kinnaird,
  Your tocher gude to pay."

" If ye gar my father sell Kinnaird,
  'Twill be a crying sin,
To tocher onie weary dwarf,
  That canna tocher win."

The lady is on to Edinbrugh,
  A' for to try the law ;
And Errol he has follow'd her ;
  His ainsell for to shaw.

O up bespak her sister,
   Whose name was Lady Ann*—
" Had I been lady o' Errol,
   Or come o' sic a clan,
I wad na in this public way
   Hae sham'd my ain gudeman."

Then up bespak a wily lord,
   He spak it wi' a sneer—
" If it be the length o' five barley-corns,
   A man he will prove here."

But up bespak dame Cathrine Carnegie,
   She was na far awa—
" Indeed, my lord, it may be sae,
   If it had awns † and a'."

Errol has got it in his will,
   To choice a maid himsel ;
And he has chosen a weel-faur'd may,
   Come in, her milk to sell.

---

* This lady is sometimes called *Jane;* but both names are
erroneous. The Earl of Southesk had only two daughters; the
heroine of the ballad, and Elizabeth, who married *first* James,
second Earl of Annandale, and *secondly* David, Viscount Stormont.

    † *Awns*—beards of barley.

" Look up, look up, my weel faur'd may,
  Look up, and think na shame ;
I'll gie to thee five hundred merk,
  To bear to me a son."

He's tane the lassie by the han',
  And led her up the green ;
And twenty times he kissed her
  Afore his lady's een.

Whan they war laid in the proof-bed,
  And a' the lords looking on ;
Then a' the fifteen vow'd and swore,
  That Errol was a man.

But they hae keepit this lassie,
  Three quarters o' a year ;
And at the end o' nine lang mouths,
  A son to him she bare.

And there was three thairbut, thairbut,
  And there was three thairben ;
And three looking oure the window hie—
  Crying, " Errol's prov'd a man !

And whan the word gaed through the town,
  The sentry gied a cry—

" O fair befa' you ! Errol, now,
 For ye hae won the day."

" O I'll tak aff my robes o' silk,
 And fling them·oure the wa' ; ,
And I'll gae maiden hame again—
 Awa, Errol, awa !"

" Tak hame your dochter, Sir Carnegie,
 And put her til the glen,
For Errol canna please her,
 Nor nane o' Errol's men."

And ilka day her plate was laid, .
 Bot an a siller spune ;
And three times cried oure Errol's yett,—
 " Lady Errol come and dine."*

And the rantin o't and the dantin o't,
 According as ye ken ;
And the thing ye ca' the dantin o't—
 Lady Errol lies her leen.

---

* *Var.*—Seven years the trencher sat ,
 And seven years the spune ;
Seven years the servant cried—
 " Lady Errol, come and dine."

_____

THE ASTROLOGER.

THERE was a handsome 'Strologer
  In London town did dwell,
For telling maids their fortune,
  There was few could him excell.
        With my fal, lal, &c.

A pretty maid, as I heard said,
  Unto his lodgings went,
All for to get her fortune read,
  And that was her intent.
        With my fal, lal, &c.

In asking for this cunning man,
  Was answered by his maid—
" He's up into his chamber"—
  " Go, call him down," she said.
        With my fal, lal, &c.

" If you would read my fortune right,
   I willing would you pay"—
" There's no doubt but I can, fair maid,
   Will ye walk up stairs with me ?"
          With my fal, lal, &c.

" I will not walk up stairs with you,
   Nor any man indeed ;"—
And she spoke with as much modesty,
   As if she'd been a maid.
          With my fal, lal, &c.

" You may be as nimble as you're able,
   For I have not time to stay ;
You may be as nimble as you're able,
   For I'm but a servant may."
          With my fal, lal, &c.

" I know your but a servant may,
   I know you're not a maid !
And it's time ye were wed, fair may,
   For ye are the ranting blade.
          With my fal, lal, &c.

Deny it not, fair may," he says,
   " For I know it to be so,

That you lay with your master,
  Not many nights ago.
        With my fal, lal, &c.

Deny it not, fair maid, he said,
  For it makes your case the worse,
For you got a crown from him last night,
  And you have it in your purse.
        With my fal, lal, &c.

KEMPY* KAYE.

This ludicrous production seems to be a parody on a passage in the ancient metrical romance of "The marriage of Sir Gawaine;" of which a fragment is published in Percy's Reliques. Sir Kaye, for his unknightly disrespect of the " lothely lady," whom he so uncourteously anathematised, is here transformed into her ardent lover ; but unfortunately the termination of their loves remains unknown, as the ballad breaks off abruptly at the most interesting point. Sir Kaye, however, appears not to have been terrified at the " snout " of the lady, or "in doubt " of his kiss ; for he seems, if we judge from the " extreme unction " he underwent, to have been literally *glued* to the lips of the loathesome lady.

Mr. Sharpe, whose opinion on such matters is deserving of the highest regard, considers this ballad to be of Danish extraction, and refers to the *Illustrations of Northern Antiquities*, p. 311, for a humourous song of the same nature, called *Sir Guncelin*, translated from the Kæmpe Viser, by Mr. Jamieson, in which all the characters are *kemps* or giants.

---

* Diminutive of *Kemp*, a champion or warrior.

KEMPY KAYE.

KEMPY KAYE is a wooing gane,
   Far far ayont the sea,
And there he met wi' auld Goling,
   His gudefather to be, be,
   His gudefather to be.

" Whar are ye gaun, O Kempy Kaye,
   Whar are ye gaun sae sune ?"
" O I am gaun to court a wife,
   And think na ye that's weel dune, dune,
   And think na ye that's weel dune ?"

" An ye be gaun to court a wife,
   As ye do tell to me,
'Tis ye sall hae my Fusome Fug,
   Your ae wife for to be, be,
   Your ae wife for to be."

" Rise up, rise up, my Fusome Fug,
　　And mak your foul face clean,
For the brawest wooer that ere ye saw
　　Is come develling*, doun the green, green,
　　Is come develling doun the green."

Up then raise the Fusome Fug,
　　To mak her foul face clean ;
And aye she curs'd her mither
　　She had na water in, in,
　　She had na water in.

She rampit† out, and she rampit in,
　　She rampit but and ben ;
The tittles and tattles‡ that hang frae her tail
　　Wad muck an acre o' land, land,
　　Wad muck an acre o' land.

She had a neis upon her face,
　　Was like an auld pat-fit ;
　　Atween her neis bot and her mou,
Was inch thick deep o' dirt, dirt,
Was inch thick deep o' dirt.

---

* *Develling*—sauntering.
† *Rampit*—pranced about in bad humour.
‡ *Tittles and tattles*—clots of dirt, such as hang on a cow's tail.

She had twa een intil her head,
  War like twa rotten plooms*,
The heavy brows hung doun her face,
  And O! I vow, she glooms, glooms,
  And O! I vow she glooms.

Ilka hair that was on her head
  Was like a heather cow ;†
And ilka louse that lookit out,
  Was like a lintseed bow, bow.‡
  Was like a lintseed bow.

Whan Kempy Kaye cam to the house,
  He lookit thro' a hole :
And there he saw the dirty drab
  Just whisking oure the coal, coal,
  Just whisking oure the coal.

He gied to her a braw silk napkin,
  Was made o' an auld horse brat* :
" I ne'er wore a silk napkin a' my life,
  But weel I wat I'se wear that, that,
  But weel I wat I'se wear that."

---

* *Plooms*—plumbs.   † *Cow*—a twig.
  ‡ *Bow*—the pericarpium of lint.

He gied to her a braw gowd ring,
  Was made frae an auld brass pan :—
" I ne'er wore a gowd ring in a' my life,
  But now I wat I'se wear ane, ane,
  But now I wat I'se wear ane."

Whan thir twa lovers had met thegither,
  O kissing to tak their fill ;
The slaver that hang atween their twa gabs
  Wad hae tether'd a ten year auld bill, bill,*
  Wad hae tether'd a ten year auld bill,

*   *   *

---

* *Bill*—the west country pron. of *bull*.

HEY THE MANTLE.

Among the numerous ancient ditties enumerated in the " Complaynt of Scotland " there occurs, *Fayr luf, lent thow me thy mantil, joy !* " The original song," says Dr. Leyden, " is probably lost ; but a ludicrous parody, in which the chorus is preserved, is well known in the south of Scotland. It begins,

> Our Guidman's away to the Mers,
>   Wi' the mantle, jo ! wi' the mantle, jo !
> Wi' his breiks on his heid, and his bonnet on his ——,
>   Wi' the merry, merry mantle o' the green, jo !"

The Editor has never seen the above version ; but the following one is still preserved in the north country. Our ancestors appear to have been very fond of the ludicrous ; many specimens of their talents for that species of composition will be found in the present collection.

XII.

HEY THE MANTLE!

Early in the morning whan the cat crew day,
   Hey the mantle! how the mantle!
Our gudeman saddl'd the bake-bread, and fast rade away
   And hey for a mantle o' the gude green hay.

Our gudeman's gane awa to the Mers,
   Hey the mantle! how the mantle!
Wi' his breeks on's head, and his bonnet on's arse,
   And hey for a mantle o' the gude green hay.

And as he gaed through thick wud, thin wud's brither,
   Hey the mantle! how the mantle!
Ilka tree stood a mile frae the ither,
   And hey for a mantle o' the gude green hay.

As he cam bye the mill door, he heard psalms singing,
    Hey the mantle! how the mantle!
As he cam bye the kirk door, he heard the meal grinding,
    And hey for a mantle o' the gude green hay.

There war four-and-twenty tailors riding on a snail,
    Hey the mantle! how the mantle!
" Ho!" quo' the foremost, "I'll be heads oure her tail,"
    And hey for a mantle o' the gude green hay.

There war four-and-twenty tailors riding on a paddock,
    Hey the mantle! how the mantle!
"Ho!" says the foremost, "we'll haud her at the gallop,"
    And hey for a mantle o' the gude green hay.

There war four-and-twenty tailors playing at the ba',
    Hey the mantle! how the mantle!
Up started headless and took it frae them a',
    And hey for a mantle o' the gude green hay.

———

Four-and-twenty cripple tailors, riding on a snail;
 This lies leal on my thrawn sang,
" O," says the foremost, " we'll a' be oure the tail,
 And we'll a' be thrawn or we gang O."

Four-and-twenty blind men playin' at the ba;
 This, &c.
Up cam the foremost and took it frae them a',
 And, &c.

Four-and-twenty young maids swimming in a pool;
 This, &c.
" O," says the youngest, " we'll a' be drown'd or Yule,
 And, &c.

Four-and-twenty auld wives skinning at a whale,
  This, &c.
Up cam the foremost, and took it by the tail,
  And, &c.

Four-and-twenty dirten brats pelting at a frog;
  This, &c.
Up cam the foremost, says, "wha's the greatest rogue,
  And, &c.

Four-and-twenty windmills running in a burn;
  This, &c.
By cam the fairies and garr'd them a' turn,
  And, &c.

Four-and-twenty young men wi' faces like the moon,
  This, &c.
Let ony ane do better, for noo my sang is dune,
  And, &c.

THE MAN IN THE MOON.

The following ditty, particularizing various optical illusions, and strange absurdities, to which a man in his cups is subject, through the medium of seeing double, reminds us of the eccentricities of the "drunken *menyie* of old Sir Thom o' Lyne:"

> Jock looked at the sun, and cried " fire, fire, fire ;"
> Tom stabled his keffel in Birkendale mire ;
> Jem started a calf, and halloo'd for a stag ;
> Will mounted a gate-post instead of his nag :
>   For all our men were very, very merry,
>   And all our men were drinking.
> There were two men of mine,
> Three men of thine,
> And three that belonged to old Sir Thom o' Lyne ;
> As they went to the ferry, they were very, very merry,
>   For all our men were drinking.

THE MAN IN THE MOON.

I saw the man in the moon,
    Wha's fou, wha's fou?
I saw the man in the moon,
    Wha's fou, now, my jo?
I saw the man in the moon,
    Driving tackets in his shoon;
And we're a' blind-drunk, bousing jolly fou, my jo.

I saw a sparrow draw a harrow,
    Wha's fou, wha's fou?
I saw a sparrow draw a harrow,
    Wha's fou, now, my jo?
I saw a sparrow draw a harrow,
    Up the Bow and down the Narrow,
And we're a' blind drunk, bousing jolly fou, my jo.

I saw a pyet haud the pleuch,
    Wha's fou, wha's fou ?
I saw a pyet haud the pleuch,
    Wha's fou, now, my jo?
I saw a pyet haud the pleuch,
    And he whissel'd weel eneuch ;
And we're a' blind drunk, bousing jolly fou, my jo.

I saw a wran kill a man,
    Wha's fou, wha's fou ?
I saw a wran kill a man,
    Wha's fou now, my jo ?
I saw a wran kill a man,
    Wi' a braidsword in his han' ;
And we're a' blind drunk, bousing jolly fou, my jo.

I saw a sheep shearing corn,
    Wha's fou, wha's fou ?
I saw a sheep shearing corn,
    Wha's fou, now, my jo ?
I saw a sheep shearing corn,
    Wi' the heuck about his horn ;
And we're a' blind drunk, bousing jolly fou, my jo.

I saw a puggie wearing boots,
    Wha's fou, wha's fou ?

I saw a puggie wearing boots,
  Wha's fou, now, my jo ?
I saw a puggie wearing boots,
  And he had but shachled cutes ;
And we're a' blind drunk, bousing jolly fou, my jo.

I saw a ram wade a dam,
  Wha's fou, wha's fou ?
I saw a ram wade a dam,
  Wha's fou, now, my jo ?
I saw a ram wade a dam,
  Wi' a mill-stane in his han' ;
And we're a' blind drunk, bousing jolly fou, my jo.

I saw a louse chace a mouse,
  Wha's fou, wha's fou ?
I saw a louse chace a mouse,
  Wha's fou, now, my jo ?
I saw a louse chace a mouse,
  Out the door, and round the house ;
And we're a' blind drunk, bousing jolly fou, my jo.

I saw a sow sewing silk,
  Wha's fou, wha's fou ?
I saw a sow sewing silk,
  Wha's fou, now, my jo ?

I saw a sow sewing silk,

And the cat was kirning milk ;

And we're a' blind drunk, bousing jolly fou, my jo.

I saw a dog shoe a horse,

   Wha's fou, Wha's fou ?

I saw a dog shoe a horse,

   Wha's fou, now, my jo ?

I saw a dog shoe a horse,

   Wi' the hammer in his a—e;

And we're a' blind drunk, bousing jolly fou, my jo.

I saw an eel chase the deil,

   Wha's fou, wha's fou ?

I saw an eel chase the deil,

   Wha's fou, now, my jo ?

I saw an eel chase the deil,

   Round about the spinning wheel,

And we're a' blind drunk, bousing jolly fou, my jo.

XV.

THE SHOEMAKER.

" Shoemaker, shoemaker, are ye within?
    A fal a falladdie fallee;
Hae ye got shoes that will fit me so trim,
    For a kiss in the morning early?"

" O fair may come in and see,
    A fal, &c.
I've got but ae pair, and I'll gie them to thee
    For a kiss in the morning early.

He's tane her in behind the bench,
    A fal, &c.
And there he has fitted his own pretty wench
    With a kiss in the morning early.

Whan twenty weeks war come and gane,
    A fal, &c.
This maid cam back to her shoemaker then,
    For a kiss in the morning early.

"O," says she, "I can't spin at a wheel,"
    A fal, &c.
"If ye can't spin at a wheel, ye may spin at a rock,
For I go not to slight my ain pretty work
    That was done in the morning early."

Whan twenty weeks war come and gone,
    A fal, &c.
This maid she brought forth a braw young son,
    For her kiss in the morning early.

" O says her father, we'll cast it out,
    A fal, &c.
It is but the shoemaker's dirty clout,
    It was got in a morning early."

O says her mother, we'll keep it in.
    A fal, &c.
It was born a prince, and it may be a king,*
    It was got in a morning early.

---

    * *King Crispin* I presume.

' Whan other maids gang to the ball,
     A fal,' &c.
She must sit and dandle her shoemaker's awl,
    For her kiss in the morning early.

Whan other maids gang to their tea,
     A fal, &c.
She must sit at hame and sing balillalee,
    For her kiss in the morning early.

THE MAIDEN'S DREAM.

ONE nicht as I lay on my bed
　　With all my joys in extasie,
And naething but my maidenhead
　　Was for to bear me companie.

One cam to me, both tall and young,
　　And unto me great love did show;
My yielding heart consented straight,
　　Then love in every vein did flow.

He talk'd to me of a married life,
　　And then bade me appoint the day;
My yielding heart consented straight,
　　I had na power to say him nay.

And whan the happy morning cam,
   I thocht how bless'd a maid was I,
To see me go along the streets,
   Wi' my bride-maidens in clean array.

And whan to church I was brought then,
   In cam to me my sweet bridegroom—
But friends believe me, sair it griev'd me,
   Whan I found it was but a dream !

And whan to dinner I was set doun,
   At the table-head wi' mickle pride,
To see the smiling bowl gae round—
   " Here's a health to you, my bonny bride !"

And after dinner I was conveyed
   Into a large and spacious hall ;
For there the sweetest music play'd,
   Till we did for nicht-bouer call.

And whan to bed I was brought then,
   In cam to me my sweet bridegroom ;
But friends believe me, sair it griev'd me,
   Whan I found it was but a dream !

I wish my dream had lasted long,
   Then I had more delighted been ;
But whan I awoke, sair to my hurt,
   Alas ! I found it was but a dream !

THE COVERING BLUE.

" My father he locks the doors at nicht,
    My mither the keys carries ben, ben ;
There's naebody dare gae out, she says,
    And as few dare come in, in,
    And as few dare come in."

" I will mak a lang ladder,
    Wi' fifty steps and three, three,
I will mak a lang ladder,
    And lichtly come doun to thee, thee,
    And lichtly come doun to thee."

He has made a lang ladder,
    Wi' fifty steps and three, three,
And he has made a lang ladder,
    And lichtly come doun the lum, lum,
    And lichtly come doun the lum.

They had na kiss'd, nor lang clappit,
   (As lovers do whan they meet, meet)
Till the auld wife says to the auld mau,—
   " I hear some body speak, speak,
   I hear some body speak.

I dreamed a dream sin late yestreen,
   And I'm fear'd my dream be true, true;
I dream'd that the rattens cam thro' the wa'
   And cuttit the covering blue, blue,
   And cuttit the covering blue.

Ye'll rise, ye'll rise, my auld gudeman,
   And see gin this be true, true,"—
" If ye're wanting rising, rise yoursel,
   For I wish the auld chiel had you, you,
   For I wish the auld chiel had you."

" I dream'd a dream sin late yestreen,
   And I'm fear'd my dream be true, true;
I dream'd that the clerk, and our ae dother,
   War rowed in the covering blue, blue,
   War rowed in the covering blue.

Ye'll rise, ye'll rise, my auld gudeman,
   And see gin this be true, true,"—

" If ye're wanting rising, rise yoursel,
  For I wish the auld chiel had you, you,
  For I wish the auld chiel had you."

But up she raise, and but she gaes,
  And she fell into a gin, gin ;
He gied the tow a clever tit,
  That brocht her out at the lum, lum,
  That brocht her out at the lum.

" Ye'll rise, ye'll rise, my auld gudeman,
  Ye'll rise and come to me now, now ;
For him that ye've gien me sae lang til,
  I fear he has gotten me now, now,
  I fear he has gotten me now."

" The grip that he's gotten, I wish he may haud,
  And never lat it gae, gae ;
For atween you and your ae dother,
  I rest neither nicht nor day, day,
  I rest neither nicht nor day."

—

THE MUIR HEN.

The bonnie muir hen gaed down the den,
  To gather in her cattle ;
I bent my bow to fire at her,
  But I could never ettle.

(Ch.) Sing archie owdum diddledum dow,
  Sing archie owdum dowdum,
  Sing archie owdum diddledum dow dum,
  Diddle dum, diddle dum dow dum.

And ae the nearer that I cam,
  Its ae she sang the louder—
" I loe the young men wondrous weel,
  But they do want the pouder."

" O haud your tongue, fair maid, he says,
  And dinna gie me the scorn ;
Ye dinna ken whare we may meet
  Wi' pouder in my horn."

The next time that he did her meet,
  Was doun amang the corn ;—
" How do you do, fair maid, he says,
  There's pouder in my horn."

He's tane her by the milk-white hand,
  And on the leys he's laid her,
And there he's tane his wills o' her,
  Before he let her gather.

And when he let her up again,
  And she saw the leys about her ;—
" I'll rue the day that ever I said,
  The young men wanted pouder."

Whan twenty weeks war come an gane,
  This maid began to weary ;
And ae she cried, " My back, my back,
  I' the drear time o' the yearie.

And whan he cam into the ha,'
  And saw the wives about her—
" Ye're na sae ill's I wish'd ye yet,
  Whan ye said I wanted pouder.

But I thought my gun would me misgie,
  Whan I had her on my shouther,
Tho' my flint was soft and fired not,
  'Twas an for want o' pouder,"

———

Widows are sour, and widows are dour,
   And widows are aye faint hearted;
But lasses are kind, wi' courtship in mind,
   Wi' money into their pocket.

Money into their pocket, he says,
   And gowd into their coffer;
But Jeanie Beddie's better than that,
   She has three lads in her offer.

Jamie Jack he loves her weel,
   But Jock Mouat loes her better,
But Willie Anderson will gae mad,
   If that he dinna get her.

Jeanie lay sick on the bleaching green,
   And Willie's leg lay oure her;
He could na get a kiss o' his love,
   For Burley glowring oure her.

O gin Burley was lying sick,
   And never to get better,
Syne I wad get a kiss o' my love,
   And nane ken o' the matter.

But gin ye had been wi' me yestreen,
   Ye wad hae riven for laughter,
To see the loun get oure the crown,
   For kissing o' Jeanie Clerk's dochter.

BONNIE BUCHAIRN.

Quhilk o' ye lasses will go to Buchairn ?
Quhilk o' ye lasses will go to Buchairn ?
Quhilk o' ye lasses will go to Buchairn ?
And be the gudewife o' bonnie Buchairn ?

I'LL no hae the lass wi' the gowden locks,
Nor will I the lass wi' the bonnie breast-knots,
But I'll hae the lass wi' the shaif o' bank notes,
To plenish the toun o' bonnie Buchairn,
　　　Quhilk o' ye, &c.

I'll get a thigging frae auld John Watt,
And I'll get ane frae the Lady o' Glack,

And I'll get anither frae honest John Gray,
For keeping his sheep sae lang on the brae.
    Sae quhilk, &c,

Lassie, I am gaun to Lawren'-fair,*
" Laddie, what are ye gaun to do there ?"
To buy some ousen, some graith, and some bows,
To plenish the toun o' Buchairn's knows.

   Then, some o' ye, lasses, maun go to Buchairn,
   Some o' ye, lasses, maun go to Buchairn,
   Now, some o' ye, lasses, maun go to Buchairn,
   And be the gudewife o' bonnie Buchairn.

---

* *Lawren'-fair,* a market held at Lawrence-kirk, in Mearns-
shire.

XXI.

———

It fell on a morning, a morning in May,
My father's cows they all went astray,
I loutit me doun, and the heather was gay,
   And a burr stack to my apron.

O ! ance my apron it was side,
But now my knees it will scarcely hide,
And O the grief that I do bide,
   Whan I look to my apron.

O ! ance my apron it was new,
But now it's gotten anither hue,
But now it's gotten anither hue,
   There's a braw lad below my apron

I saw my father ou the stair,
Kaiming doun his yellow hair,
Says,—" What is that ye've gotten there,
  Sae weel row'd aneath your apron ?"

It's no a vagabond, nor yet a loon—
He's the rarest stay-maker in a' the toun,
And he's made a stomacher to bear up my goun,
  And I row'd it aneath my apron.

I saw my mither on the stair,
Kaiming done her yellow hair,
Says—" What's that ye've gotten there ;
  Sae weel row'd aneath your apron ?

It is my mantle and my shirt,
I had na will to daidle it,
I had na will to daidle it,
  And I row'd it aneath my apron.

As I was walking up the street,
Wi' silver slippers on my feet,
O ! aye my friends I'd ill will to meet,
  And my braw lad row'd in my apron.

———

First there cam whipmen, and that not a few,
And there cam bonnetmen following the pleugh ;
But he was a brisk farmer, he was brisk and airy,
Monie times courted, but never to marry :
    Court her, court her, court her, and leave her,
    O sic a pity that they should grieve her.

The next was a merchantman out o' the town,
She washed his stockings and dichted his shoon ;
And aye for the courting the lassie was keen,
The lassie was keen, and the laddie was airy,
Monie times courted, but never to marry :
    Court her, court her, court her, and leave her,
    O sic a pity that they should grieve her.

   *   *   *   *

XXIII.

LAIRD O' LEYS.

This ballad relates to a *faux pas* of one of the Bur-
nets of Leys, in Mearns-shire; but which of them I know
not.

THE Laird o' Leys is to London gane,
    He was baith full and gawdie;
For he shod his steed wi' siller guid,
    And he's play'd the ranting laddie.

He hadna been in fair London
    A twalmonth and a quarter,
Till he met wi' a weel-faur'd may,
    Wha wish'd to ken how they ca'd him.

" They ca' me this, and they ca' me that,
    And they're easy how they've ca'd me;
But whan I'm at hame on bonnie Deeside,
    They ca' me the ranting laddie."

" Awa wi' your jesting, Sir," she said,
　" I trow you're a ranting laddie,
But something swells atween my sides,
　And I maun ken how they ca' thee."

" They ca' me this, and they ca' me that,
　And their easy how they ca' me :
The Baron o' Leys my title is,
　And Sandy Burnet they ca' me."

" Tell down, tell down, ten thousand crowns,
　Or ye maun marry me the morn,
Or headit and hangit ye sall be,
　For ye sanna gie me the scorn."

" My head's the thing I canna weel want ;
　My lady she loves me dearlie ;
Nor yet hae I means ye to maintain—
　Alas ! for the lying sae near thee."

But word's gane down to the Lady o' Leys,
　That the Baron had got a babie ;
" The waurst o' news," my lady she said,
　I wish I had hame my laddie.

But I'll sell off my jointure-house,
   Tho' na mair I sud be a ladie;
I'll sell a', to my silken goun,
   And bring hame my ranting laddie."

So she is on to London gane,
   And she paid the money on the morn;
She paid it doun, and brought him hame,
   And gien them a' the scorn.

TAM BARROW.

'Twas in the month of Februar,
    Whan Tam was first a widower;
Thir words I will rehearse to you
    About auld Tam Barrow.

His mukle-coat, his hairy wig,
    O vow! he lookit dreary,
He wad hae put ye in a fricht,
    Gin ance he had cam near ye.

He was na widower lang ago,
    Till he grew tap-and-teerie;
And he has thro' the kintry gane,
    To seek anither dearie.

He wash'd his face, he kaim'd his hair,
　　He was a lusty fallow,
And a' the lasses blinkit blythe,
　　At auld Tam Barrow.

A' the lasses blinkit blythe,
　　But few o' them had tocher,
Na sooner did they gie consent,
　　Of them he spier'd their coffer.

But he's to a rich widow gane,
　　That had baith white and yellow,—
Will ye consent to marry me?
　　Says auld Tam Barrow.

Your children I will put to school,
　　Yoursel I will haud easy;
Ye'll sit richt warm at my fireside,
　　Whan you grow auld and crazy.

But he was na married lang ago,
　　Till he began to weary;—
Pack aff your children and begone,
　　Says auld Tam Barrow.

———

Johnie cam to our toun,
To our toun, to our toun,
Johnie cam to our toun,
The body wi' thet ye;
And O as he kittl'd me,
Kittl'd me, kittl'd me,
O as he kittl'd me—
But I forgot to cry.

He gaed thro' the fields wi' me,
The fields wi' me, the fields wi' me,
He gaed thro' the fields wi' me,
And doun amang the rye;
Then O as he kittl'd me,
Kittl'd me, kittl'd me,
Then O as he kittl'd me—
But I forgot to cry.

T

THE RAM OF DIRAM.

As I cam in by Diram,
  Upon a sunshine day,
I there did meet a ram, Sir,
  He was baith gallant and gay.

  And a hech, hey, a-Diram,
    A-Diram, a-Dandalee;
  He was the gallantest ram, Sir,
    That ere mine eyes did see.

He had four feet to stand upon,
  As ye sall understand;
And ilka fit that the ram had
  Wad hae cover'd an acre o' land.

The woo that grew on the ram's back,
  Was fifty packs o' claith ;
And for to mak a lee, Sir,
  I wad be very laith.

The horns that war on the ram's head,
  Were fifty packs o' speens ;
And for to mak a lee, Sir,
  I never did it eence.

This ram was fat behind, Sir,
  And he was fat before ;
This ram was ten yards lang, Sir,
  Indeed he was no more. ·

The tail that hang at the ram,
  Was fifty fadom and an ell,
And it was sauld at Diram,
  To ring the market-bell.

  And a hech, hey, a-Diram,
    A-Diram, a-dandalee ;
  He was the gallantest ram, Sir,
    That ere my eyes did see.

XXVII.

THE KNAVE.

I GAED to the market,
  As an honest woman shou'd,
The knave followed me,
  As ye ken a knave wou'd.

  And a knave has his knave tricks,
    Aye where'er he be,
  And I'll tell ye bye and bye,
    How the knave guided me.

I boucht a pint ale,
  As an honest woman shou'd ;
The knave drank it a',
  As ye ken a knave wou'd.

I cam my ways hame,
  As an honest woman shou'd,
The knave follow'd me,
  As ye ken a knave wou'd.

I gied him cheese and bread,
　As an honest woman shou'd ;
The knave ate it a',
　As ye ken a knave wou'd.

I gaed to my bed,
　As an honest woman shou'd ;
The knave follow'd me,
　As ye ken a knave wou'd.

I happen'd to be wi bairn,
　As an honest woman shou'd ;
The knave ran awa,
　As ye ken a knave wou'd.

I paid the nourice fee,
　As an honest woman wou'd ;
The knave got the widdie,
　As ye ken a knave shou'd.

　　And a knave has his knave tricks,
　　Aye where e'er he be,
　　And I've tamed you now
　　How the knave guided me.

———

There was a little wee bridelie,
 In Pitcarles toun,
 In Pitcarles toun ;
There was few fowk bidden to it,
 And as few fowk did come,
 And as few fowk did come.

There was nae mair meat at it,
 Than a sheep's head but the tongue,
 Than a sheep's head but the tongue:
And aye the bride she cried—
 I pray ye lads eat some,
 I pray ye lads leave some.

There was nae drink but a soup
 I' the boddom o' a tun,
 I' the boddom o' a tun ;
And aye the bride she cried,
 I pray ye lads drink some,
 I pray ye lads leave some.

There was nae music but a pipe,
  And the pipe wanted the drone,
  And the pipe wanted the drone;
And aye the bride she cried—
  I pray ye lads dance some,
  I pray ye lads dance some.

The bridegroom gaed thro' the reel,
  And his breeks cam trodling doun,
  And his breeks cam trodling doun;
And aye the bride she cried—
  Tie up your leathern whang,*
  Tie up your leathern whang.

The bride gaed till her bed,
  The bridegroom wadna come,
  The bridegroom wadna come;
And aye the bride she cried—
  I kent this day wad come,
  I kent this day wad come.

---

* Before the invention of *braces*, the nether garments were usually supported by a leathern belt round the waist.

—

THE MAUTMAN.

THIS coarse production is a different, if not an older version of *The Mautman*, published in Herd's Collection.

The Mautman comes on Munanday,
    And vow but he craves sair ;—
Now gie me my sack and my siller,
    Or maut ye're ne'er get mair,

    Bring a' your maut to me,
    Bring a' your maut to me ;
    My draff ye'll get for ae pund ane,
    Tho' a' my jockies* should dee.

---

* *Jockies*—Pigs !

She's tane the chappin stoup,
   And p——d it to the ee—
" O come, gudeman, and prie
   Sic maut as ye've gien me."—

" The maut is very gude maut,
   An it hadna been brewn sae het,"—
" O how can it otherwise be,
   Whan it's new come out o' the fat.*

Now, hark ye, hark ye, kimmer,
   And I will tell ye how
There cam to our house yestreen,
   A curst unruly crew :

A curst unruly crew,
   And they did breed a quarrel,
They gaed doun to the cellar below,
   And they pierc'd my dochter's barrel :

They pierced my dochter's barrel,
   And syne ran awa wi' the cock,
And aye, and aye sin syne,
   My lassie rins lowss † i' the dock.

---

    * *Fat*—vat.   † *Lowss*—loose.

Some say kissing's a sin,
   But I think its nane ava,
For kissing was won'd * in the warld,
   Whan there was but only twa.

If it wasna lawfu',
   Lawyers wadna allow it;
If it was na holy,
   Ministers wadna do it.

If it wasna modest,
   Maidens wadna tak it;
And if it was na plenty,
   Puir fowk wad na get it.

   Bring a' your maut to me,
     Bring a' your maut to me ;
     My draff ye'll get for ae pund ane,
     Tho' a' my jockies should dee.

---

* *Won'd*—known, an oblique sense of *dwelt.*

A

New Book

of

Old Ballads.

Edinburgh.

m.dccc.xliv.

" I love a ballad but even too well ; if it be doleful matter, merrily set down, or a very pleasant thing indeed, and sung lamentably."   WINTER'S TALE.

THE chief attraction of the present Collection consists in the recovery of early versions of two or three popular Scotish Ballads, which, passing through the *barber*-ous hands of Allan Ramsay, or other renovators of ancient garments, have, like the silk stockings of Sir John Cutlar, retained very few portions of their original texture.

Thus " Scornful," (termed by Ramsay " Bonny") Nancy, is essentially different from the song introduced to the notice of the public in the Tea-Table Miscellany, and the recovery of the original ballad establishes, in spite of Mr. Stenhouse's observations to the contrary,* that the lady had not escaped intact from the poet's embraces. It is singular that the dialect used in the original is peculiar to Aberdeenshire, a circumstance which would tend to fix the locality there, and lead to an inference that the author belonged to that district of country.

* See page 12.

The modern edition of " No Dominies for me Lady," has not more than three or four lines of the one here printed, and it may be noticed that it also differs very essentially from an original, perhaps unique, broadside of the Ballad, in possession of the Editor. It has been suggested that the word should be *Laddie*, not Lady—but as the latter occurs in the MS. as well as in the broadside, it was not deemed expedient to adopt the emendation, however ingenious.

It is unnecessary to go over the list, so the Reader is referred for further observation to the short Prefatory Introduction prefixed to each Ballad. It is proper, however, to give some account of the MS. whence the first ten Ballads have been taken. It is in the hand-writing of William Hamilton, younger of Airdrie, and forms a few leaves, perfixed to a small oblong duodecimo, containing almost entirely Notes of Lectures on Physic by Professor Tran of the University of Glasgow, from 1699 to 1700 ; the remaining two or three leaves consisting of " a Catalogue of Books left at Airdrie by W. H.," and a memorandum of books lent.

The manuscript is now in possession of the great-grandson of the former owner, Sir William Hamilton of Preston, Bart., who kindly gave the uncontrolled. use of it to the Editor. The Ballads were evidently written down by Mr. Hamilton when at College, and probably when recording them, he little imagined that they would eventually turn out to be the more interesting portion of his MS. The rest of the Collection consists of a few Ballads and Fragments, two or three of which were taken down from recitation, and the remainder from scarce broadsides.

It may here be remarked, that the Ballad entitled the " Cardinal's Coach Couped" refers to the Toleration Act, by which the persecuted Episcopal Clergy got some relief. The case of the Reverend Mr. Greenshields, which had been determined in favour of the Presbyterian Inquisition by the Court of Session, was taken by Appeal to the House of Lords, and there reversed. The disclosures attendant upon the discussion of this suit revealed to those in England the intolerable hardships to which their brethren in Scotland were exposed, and the Legislature interfered in their behalf. For an account of the whole proceedings, the Reader may be referred to the valuable History of the Scotish Episcopal Church from the Revolution, by John Parker Lawson, M.A. Edinburgh, 1843, p. 196. By the Cardinal, Principal

Carstairs, the head of the Presbyterian party is meant; it was the sobriquet usually applied to him by the Jacobites.

Some of the lines may shock the fastidious, but as the Volume is intended for private circulation, and as the impression is limited to SIXTY COPIES, [ONE COPY UPON VELLUM printed exclusively for the Collection of Vellum Books in the matchless Library of JOSEPH WALTER KING EYTON, Esquire, of Elgin Villa, Leamington, Warwickshire,] any apology for giving the different versions without castration seems unnecessary.

J. M.

3, LONDON STREET,
November 1843.

CONTENTS.

U

The Order of Singing Oct 711

Ile gar our gudeman trow
That Ile sell the ladle
If he winna buy to me
If he winna buy to me
Ile gar our gudeman trow
That Ile sell the ladle
If he winna buy to me
A bonny new side saddle.
To ride to Kirk & market
and round about the town
Stan' about ye fisher jads
Stan' about ye fisher jads
To ride to Kirk & market
and round about the town
Stan about ye fisher jads
and gie my joan o'er

A NEW BOOK OF OLD BALLADS.

I.

𝔅𝔩𝔭𝔱𝔥𝔢 𝔍𝔬𝔠𝔨𝔦𝔢.

Blyth Jocky is given in Johnson's Scotish Musical Museum, vol. i. No. 24, with different and very inferior words. In the notes, p. 23, it is said both " the air and words of this Anglo-Scotish Song" are comparatively modern.   It was inserted in the first edition of Horsfield's Songster's Companion.   2 vols. 12mo. London, 1770.

1

BLYTH Jockie young and gay,
   He's all my heart's delight—
He's all my thoughts by day,
   And in my dreams by night.
If from the lad I be,
Its winter then with me;
But while he's with me here,
Its summer all the year.

2

When Jockie and I did meet
 First in the shady grove,
How kindly he did me treat,
 And sweetly talk't of love.
Ye are the lass, said he,
That stoll my heart from me.
Come ease me of my pain,
And doe not me disdain.

3

I'm blyth when Jockie comes,
 Sad when he goes away;
It's night when Jockie gloums,
 But when he smiles it's day.
Where e're we meet I pant,
I colour, sigh, and faint,
What lass that would be kind,
Can better tell her mind.

4

He was a bonnie lad
 As ever I did see,
He made my heart soe glad,
 When first he courted me.

I could not well deny,
But soon I did comply.
Soe Jockie promis'd me,
That he would faithful be.

5

Jockie did promise me,
    That he would still prove true,
But to my grief, I fear,
    He hath bid me adieu.
Jockie and I did play,
And pass the time away;
But now he's false, forsworn,
And left me here to mourn.

6

Now Jockie hath a love,
    That is more rich than I,
He doth soe cruel prove,
    To shun my company,
And if I chance to meet,
My Jockie in the street,
He will not stop nor stay
But proudly goes away.

7

My heart is like to break,
  Since he is soe unkind,
What course then shall I take,
  To ease my troubled mind.
I sigh, I sob, I mourn,
I dayly rage and burn,
But yet this cruel he
Laughs at my misery.

8

Once in a month, he sends
  A letter unto me
Vowing he still intends,
  To love me heartily.
But when I come in place,
And doe behold his face,
Then he noe notice takes,
Which makes my heart to break.

II.

Lady Arrol's Lament.

This Ballad is not to be found in any of the Collections. Who the Lady Arrol (Errol) may be is not very easy to say. There was a very naughty lady of the Carnegie family that married the Earl of Errol, and attempted his life. Her cause of dislike will be found in a note prefixed to a ballad on the subject, printed by C. K. Sharpe, Esq. in his Ballad Book, p. 89.

1

WHEN I'm absent from the lass that I love,
    I fain would resolve to love noe more;
My reason would my flames remove,
    But my love-sick heart doth still adore.
My weak endeavours are all in vain,
    They vanish so soon as she returns;
And with a sigh relapse again,
    Into a raging fever burns.

2

To the rocks and the hills I make my moan,
  To whom my passion I doe tell,—
I fancied that I heard her moan
  ˙Her echoes back I lov'd soe well,—
Leave off your passion, and do not pursue,
  Lest it should end in misery;
For shee is in love, but not with you,
  Why should ye then despair and dye.

3

We may change countrey, and not move
Our constancy and fervent love,
Though ye see ourselves ye know not our minde,
We may be absent and yet kind;
But I vow to the, and (the) world shall see,
That absence shall never alter me,
My dearest dear doe ye the same,
We're parted, but we'l meet again.

4

My dearest let nothing trouble your heart,
  For here I am returned again,
In order to cure that killing smart,
  Whereof ye often did complain,

It's true I was banish'd from my love,
　Which was great sorrow and grief to me,
But now I shall ever loyal prove,
　Soe long as I keep my liberty.

5

Thou art my true and entire friend,
　My chamber and all I have is thine,
There is noe bad thoughts shall me offend,
　Thy love hath win this heart of mine.
Dry up your sighs and tears shee says,
　And bid all sorrows and cares adieu,
Though fortune a while did us divide,
　Yet I fancy none in the world but you.

III.

No Dominies for me Lady.

In the new edition of Johnson's Musical Museum, vol. v. 504, there is a copy of a ballad entitled " No Dominies for me, Laddie," said to be taken from Yair's Charmer, vol. ii. p. 347. Edin. 1751.   Ritson, who inserted it in his collection, was unable to discover the tune ; but the late James Balfour, Esq. Accountant in Edinburgh, communicated the original melody, and it has been given in the first named publication.

It is said to have been written by the late Rev. Nathaniel Mackie, Minister of Cross-Michael, who died on the 26th January 1781, aged 66, but the Editor has a broadside of the original ballad, printed certainly not later than 1700, and the copy from the Hamilton MS. is at least as early in date.

In Buchan's Gleanings of Scarce Old Ballads, the Rev. John Forbes, Minister of Deer, is said to be the author. He died in 1769, in the 80th year of his age.   He must therefore have been eleven years of age in 1700—the date of the Hamilton MS.—a fact which militates against the claim of authorship set up for him.

Perhaps one or other of these reverend gentlemen may have had a hand in altering the original ballad, which is now for the first time printed.

I

No Dominies for me Lady, no Dominies for me,

For books and gouns will all goe doun,

No Dominies for me,

They can court and complement,
        But they ne're conquer me Lady,
I'le keep the fifth commandement;
        No Dominies for me Lady.

2

My parents will not give consent,
        To match with Dominies Lady,
Soe I'le keep the fifth commandement;
        No Dominies for me Lady.

3

Stipends are uncertain rents
        For lady's conjunct fee Lady.
Ministers make poor testaments;
        No Dominies for me Lady.

4

Lairds will take the place Lady,
        Both at dore and mass Lady.
Lairds must sit, chaiplains must stand,
        And bow and say the grace Lady.

5

To lairds ye seem to bear respect,
        And Dominies disdain Lady;
But a Dominie may chance to be
        Your glory and your gain Lady.

6

Phisisians they your pulse can feel—
        Your fever can allay Lady;
But a Dominie can give a peil
        That can your heart betray Lady.

7

Stipends are uncertain rents I grant
        For lady's conjunct fees Lady;
But ministers scarce ever want
        Or theirs, and what would ye have Lady.

8

If revolutions they doe come,
        Into the ministry Lady;
Then Kirklands will goe back to Rome,
        And your Lairds to poverty Lady.

9

Your parents may perhaps give consent,
      To match with Dominies Lady;
Then ye the fifth commandement
      May keep, and not despise Lady.

10

But if some other things fall in,
      That they will still gainsay Lady;
Yet constancy will bear the gree,
      And true love keep alway Lady.

11

When Lairds and Gentlemen do fall
     . Into some heinous crime Lady,
Ye'll sigh, and wring these pleasant hands;
      But alace its out of time Lady.* .

* The printed broadside noticed in the preliminary remarks,
differs essentially from the copy of the ballad now printed.

IV.

Bonnie Nancy.

This ballad occurs in Ramsay's Tea-Table Miscellany,(13th Edition), 1762, p. 17.   The version is the same as that given by Herd, and Ritson.   The present copy is entirely different, and as the earliest one known is now for the first time printed.   Ramsay calls the lady *slighted* Nancy, to the tune of "The Kirk wad let me be."   Why she is designated "slighted" in place of scornful, as Herd and Ritson have it, or "Bonny" as the Hamilton MS. gives it, is not easy to see; for in place of being "slighted," she is the party who slights her would-be spouse.

It is included in the "Orpheus Caledonius," and in Johnson's Scotish Musical Mnseum, vol. 1. No. 50, under the name of "Scornful" Nancy.   Mr. C. K. Sharpe, in a note, observes, he has an ancient MS. subjoined to an early transcript of Dryden's Absalom and Achitophel, which has a better reading.   The last line of Stanza 3, makes "Shamy's" father ride "on gude shanks nagie," whereas in his MS., (in like manner with the version now printed,) the line stands,—

"He rode an ambling nagie,"

which is more in keeping with the rest of the description.

Mr. Stenhouse, says (Scotish Musical Museum, p. 54)—"This is one of the fine old and exquisitely humorous Scottish songs which has escaped the polishing file of Ramsay, and happily reached us in its simple and native garb !"

1

Nancy's to the Greenwood gain
    To hear the gowdspink shattering;
And Shamy followed her amain
    To court her with his flattering.
But a' his flattering wad nae dee,
    She scornfuly reshect him;
And fan he tid pekin to woo,
    She speert fa tid begett him.

2

Fatt ails thee at my dade, quoth hee,
    My minny or my aunty,
With croudy moudy they fed me,
    Lang kail aud ranty tanty;
And bannocks of guide gredden meal,
    Of that we had great plenty;
And noganes full of hacket kaile,
    And fow kan that was dainty.

3

Although my faither was nae laird,
    I speak it without bantrey;
He keepet ay a guid kail yeard,
    A ha hous and a pantrey.

He ware a ponet ou hims head,
　　Ane ourlar bout hims craigie ;
And to hims very dying day,
　　He rade ane ambling naigie.

4

And fatt although my minny baik
　　A bannock in here mister ;
She had a girdle and a baick-bord,
　　That she lent to her syster.
Her callour body ys a clean,
　　And fite as any linnen [lilly ?] ;
And a green plaid, it may be seen,
　　Sae shee's nae gilter jilly.

5

On her side there is great pride,
　　Of that I think nae wondra ;
She busks hersell twice in the week,
　　And three times in the Sunday.
With pity coat and mantay coat,
　　And jampy coat like lilly ;
And a green scarf to cover all,
　　Sae she's baith fair and comely.

6

Then Nancy turn'd here round about,
   With great disdain and scoru ;
And Shamie stood her iu great doubt,
   As hee had been forlorn.
Wae and vondra light on thee,
   Wad thow have bony Nancy ;
Wad thow compare thyself to me,—
   A cow's turd to a tancy ?

7

I bid thee then goe hame, Gibb Glaicks,
   John Jillets, or some other ;
Or els I fear thow gett thy paiks,
   Goe ge be wall your father.
For I have a yonker of my own,
   They call him souple Sandy ;
And well I wot he kens the gate
   To play at hough-ma-gandy.

w

V.

The Shepherd of Dona.

Termed the "Shepherd Adonis" in Ramsay's Tea-Table Miscellany, p. 115, (13th Edition), who has interpolated and
altered, to suit his own fancy, almost every stanza. It is now
given from the Hamilton MS.

It is inserted in Johnson's Musical Museum, and in the notes,
Vol. ii. p. 148, has been attributed to Sir Gilbert Elliot of
Minto, Bart. This, it is presumed, must mean the first Baronet,
the founder of the family, as the third Baronet, the author of
the celebrated song,—

    "My sheep I neglected—I broke my sheep hook,"

was not born for twenty years after the date of the Hamilton
MS.

1

THE Shepherd of Dona being wearied with sport,
To find some repose, to the woods did resort ;
He threw by his pipe, and he laid himself down,
He envy'd noe monarch, he wished for noe crown.

2

He drank of the brook, and did eat of the tree,
Injoying himself, from all trouble was free ;
He call'd for noe nymph, were she never soe fair,
He'd noe love, noe ambition, and therfor noe care.

3

But as he lay thus, in ane evening soe cleare,
A pleasant sweet voyce outreached his eare;
Which came from Arcadia, that old ancieut grove,
Where the fair nymph Elreda frequented that cove.

4

As he lay thus, [reposing] and found she was there,
He was quite confounded to see her soe fair;
He stood like a ston, not a foot he could move,
He knew not what ail'd him, but fear'd it was love.

5

That nymph she beheld him with a modest grace,
Seing somewhat majestick appear in his face ;
Till with blushing a little, to him she did say,
Oh, good shepherd what mean you, how came ye this
    way.

6

With reviving of spirits unto her he said,
I was ne'r soe surpris'd at the sight of a maid ;
Ay until I beheld thee of love I was free,
But now I'me ta'en captive my faire love by thee.

VI.

Willy and Marie.

This Jacobite production, which has considerable merit, has not,
it is believed, been hitherto printed. It is hardly necessary to
mention that it is a violent attack on William III. and his
Queen, for putting on their heads that crown which the previ-
ous wearer's infatuated bigotry had compelled him to lay down.

1

SAYS Willy, my uncle I'le beat,
I'le trip his heels over the doore :
Says Mary, brother's a cheat,
And beside he's the son of a whore.
We'l banish religion and nature
For these be noe friends in the case,
But still we will cover the matter
With vizours and masks of grace.
    Says Willie, I'le be a King,
    Says Mary, I'le be a Queen ;
    My uncle, said hee,
    My dady, said shee,
    We'l banish, and soe we shall reigne.

2

The trayterous party that murder'd
Our Grandfather Charle de Bonn,
Shall be rewarded and honour'd
For helping to banish his sone.
Thanks be to knavery and knaves,
Thanks be to presbitry and treason,
For these be the sanctify'd means
That gain'd us a croun, in good season.

> Says Willie, I'le be a King,
> Says Marie, I'le be a Queen ;
> My Uncle, said he,
> My Dady, said shee,
> We'le banish, and soe we will reigne.

3

Blest be these Independants,
That took off our Grandfather's head,
Lett them be still our defendants
And our support in our need.
For Presbitry hatched the egg,
Independants the cockatrice nourish
A crown, though begott with a plague,
We care not soe longe as we flourish.

> Says Willie, I'le be a King,
> Says Mary, I'le be a Queen ;
> My Uncle, said he,
> My Dady, said shee,
> We'le banish, and soe we shall reigne.

4

Says Mary, our father we'l honnour,
It's true said the Marmaiden elfe;
Before that a crown hurts his head,
I'le dethron him and wear it myself;
For he is old and weak,
And we are young and souple,
And fitter than he for to reigne.
[The Devil] take the couple,
    Says good old Jamy the King,
    Says good old Jamy the King.
    The heir of the crown,
    Though depriv'd [of his own],
    Is fitter than thee for to reigne.

VII.

To Danton me.

The tune taken from the first volume of Oswald's Caledonian
Pocket Companion, printed in 1740, occurs in Johnson's
Musical Museum, vol. ii. No. clxxxii., p. 176, with words by
Burns. In the notes, p. 176, the old ballad is given, extracted
from what is termed " a very rare and curious little book,"
entitled a Collection of Loyal Songs and Poems, printed in
the year 1750. There are only *three* stanzas of it. It occurs
also in Ritson.

1

WHEN I was wanton, young, and free,
I thought nothing could danton me ;
But the eighty-eight and eighty-nine,
And all the dreary years since sine ;
Retention, sess, and pole money,
Have done enough to danton mee.

2

To danton me, to danton mee,
I thought noe thing could danton mee ;
But the abdication of our King,
And Prelacy that sacred thing,
Usurping Prince and Presbytry,
Have done right much for to danton me.

3

To danton me, to danton me,
I thought noe thing could danton me ;
The abjuration of the test,
Apostles' creed and all the rest ;
Lord's Prayer and doxology.
Have done enough for to danton me.

4

But to wanton me, to wanton me,
There is yet something would wanton me ;
Our Hogen King he must goe owt,
With all his Hogen Mogen rowt,
And all the race of Presbytry,
And that I trow would wanton me.

5

Would wanton me, would wanton me,
There's yet a thing would wanton me ;
Our King restor'd to all his three
In health, peace, and prosperity ;
No cess nor press, noe Presbytry,
And that I trow would wanton me.

6

Would wanton me, would wanton me,
There is yet something would wanton me ;
To see good corn grow on the riggs
Of persecution on the whiggs ;
And a Synod sett for Assemblies,
And that truly would wanton me.

VIII.

Dool for my Eyen.

In Hogg's Jacobite Relics, vol. i. p. 66, will be found a Ballad on the Stewart side of the question, entitled " Such a Parcel of Rogues in a Nation," which consists of three Stanzas, and has considerable merit. The present appears to be the Whig retaliation, and bating one or two faulty lines, is not inferior to the Tory song.

I

Dool for my eyen that ever I have seen
    Such a parcel of rogues in a nation,
Who's only designe is to plot and combine
    For opposing a true reformation.
      But the Pope and the Turk
      Might find some easier work,
To establish their formes amang them,
      Than these who take care
      Such abuses to repair,
Such knaves 'twere no pity to hang them.

2

When the Tories and the Teagues
Had the charge of our craigs,
When the fox had the lambs in protection ;
When tyrannical power
Did our statutes devour,
When our Court from a Priest took direction.

3

When our coyn and our pow'r
Wer consign'd upon a whore,
When Hell, France, and Rome had intended
To make us their slaves,
And our houses our graves,
They'r zealots wer ne'er discontented.

4

But our Prince who withstood
To his fortune, and blood,
Our laws and religion defending,
They defame, they oppose,
They'r the worst of his foes,
They'r traytours, though loyal pretending.

5

They have settled theyr hope
On the Turke and the Pope,
With the Devil and the French to assist them ;
    But though theyr strength made them boast,
    They shall feel to theyr cost,
That he's too great a power to resist them.

6

Let them bragg what they got
From the English and Scott,
Att Aloyne, or at Agrim, or Deep too,
    Or at Landau itself,
    Though the fols fairy elf,
Had intended to catch them asleep too.

7

Could our armys fairly meet,
As it faired with the fleet,
Perhaps ye should see some disaster ;
    They should lead such a dance,
    To that Hector in France,
As our King at Aloyn did they master.

IX.

Love is the cause of my Mourning.

In Johnson's Musical Museum, Vol. 2, No. 109, will be found the
tune of " Love is the cause of my Mourning,"—the words are
entirely different from those now printed.   The version given
in the Orpheus Caledonius, (1725), Ramsay's Tea-Table Miscellany and Johnson, has been attributed to President Forbes.

1

WHEN first my poor heart, unacquainted with love,
Cupide with his bow and his arrow did move ;
Soe sweet was the wound, and soe gentle did prove,
  While as yet my poor heart was a bleeding.
I knew not what ailed me, yet something I found,
Which I ne'er found before, still the more did abound ;
[For] Strephon, I knew, [kept] watch on the ground,
  Where his milky white flocks were a feeding.

2

O Strephon the brave, the gallant, and gay,
Soe sharp are his notes, and soe sweet he doth play,
That he charms all the nymphs in the plains all the day,
  And at night he doth keep my heart burning.

O cruel that custom that forbids to reveal,

A passion soe strong and soe hard to conceal,

To the deserts I'le goe, to the plains bid farewell,

  Since love is the cause of my mourning.

        Where the sweet nightingale

        With dolful notes doth quell,

        My longsome funeral

          As shee's flying ;

    Caus tell the woods the secret Strephon tell,

    The direful account of my dying.*

  * There is evidently something wrong here, but the Editor has given the verse as it occurs in the MS. omitting one word before Strephon in the last line but one, which is illegible.

X.

Thoughtless Clora.

Thoughtless Clora is the worst in the Collection, and hardly
merits preservation.

1

Cloras full of harmless thoughts, beneath yon well she
lay,
Had love a youthful shepherd brought to pass the time
away;
She blessed to be encounter'd so, by that enamour'd
swain;
But when she rose and strove to go, he pul'd her back
again.

2

A sudden passion seized her then, and spite of her disdain,
She found a pulse in every place, and love in every
vein;
What passions this that youth betrays, in spite of all
surprize—
Don't lett me fall unless you please, and leave noe
power to rise.

3

She fainting stood and tremblingly, for fear he should
  comply;
Her lovely eyes her heart betray'd, and made her heart
  to lye;
And she who Princes had deny'd, with all their pomp
  and train,
In that unlucky minute was betray'd unto the [lucky?]
  swaine.

XI.

The Marquis of Huntley's Retreat from the Battle of Sheriffmuir.

This very clever and spirited Ballad has been introduced by
Hogg in the second volume of his Jacobite Relics from a very
imperfect manuscript copy.   The present one is taken from
the original broadside, supposed to be unique, belonging to
Mr. David Haig of the Advocates' Library.

1

FROM Bogie side to Bogie Gight,
   The Gordons all conveen'd, man,
With all their might, to battle weight,
   Together closs they join'd, man,
To set their King upon the throne,
   And to protect the church, man ;
But fy for shame ! they soon ran hame,
   And left him in the lurch, man.
      Vow as the Marquis ran,
         Coming from Dumblane, man ;
      Strabogie did beshit itself,
         And Enzie was not clean, man.
      Vow, &c.

2

Their chieftain was a man of fame,
    And doughty deeds had wrought, man,
Which future ages still shall name, .
    And tell how well he fought, man.
For when the battle did begin,
    Immediately his Grace, man,
Put spurs to Florance,* and so ran
    By all, and wan the race, man,
          Vow, &c.

3

The Marquis' horse was first sent forth,
    Glenbucket's foot to back them,
To give a proof what they were worth,
    If rebels durst attack them.
With loud huzzas to Huntly's praise,
    They near'd Dumfermling Green, man,
But fifty horse, and de'il ane mair,
    Turn'd many a Highland clan, man.
          Vow, &c.

---

* His horse so called from having been a present from the Grand
Duke of Tuscany.

4

The second chieftain of that clan,
    For fear that he should die, man,
To gain the honour of his name,
    Rais'd first the mutinie, man.
And then he wrote unto his Grace,
    The great Duke of Argyle, man,
And swore if he would grant him peace,
    The Tories he'd beguile, man.

5

The Master * with the bullie's face,
    And with the coward's heart, man.
Who never fails, to his disgrace,
    To act a traitor's part, man.
He join'd Drumboig, the greatest knave
    In all the shire of Fife, man.
He was the first the cause did leave,
    By council of his wife, man.

                    Vow, &c.

---

* Master of Sinclair, whose Court-Martial has been printed with
an exceedingly interesting preface by Sir Walter Scott, as his con-
tribution to the Roxburgh Club,—it is one of the most curious of
the Club Books. The Memoirs of the Master still, it is to be re-
gretted, remain in manuscript. [Since, under the Editorship of
David Laing and James Macknight, published by the Abbotsford
Club in 1858.]

6

A member of the tricking trade,
  An Ogilvie by name, man ;
Consulter of the grumbling club,
  To his eternal shame, man.
Who would have thought, when he came out,
  That ever he would fail, man ;
And like a fool, did eat the cow,
  And worried on the tail, man.
                    Vow, &c.

7

Meffan Smith,* at Sheriff Muir,
  Gart folk believe he fought, man ;
But well its known, that all he did,
  That day it serv'd for nought, man.
For towards night, when Mar march'd off,
  Smith was put in the rere, man ;
He curs'd, he swore, he bauld out,
  He would not stay for fear, man.
                    Vow, &c.

* David Smith was then proprietor of Methven, an estate in Perthshire. He died in 1735. Douglas, in his Baronage, terms him, " a man of good parts, great sagacity, and economy."

8

But at the first he seem'd to be
    A man of good renown, man ;
But when the grumbling work began,
    He prov'd an arrant lown, man.
Against Mar, and a royal war,
    A letter he did forge, man ;
Against his Prince, he wrote nonsense,
    And swore by Royal* George, man.
          Vow, &c.

9

At Poineth boat, Mr. Francis Stewart,†
    A valiant hero stood, man ;
In acting of a royal part,
    Cause of the royal blood, man.
But when at Sheriff Moor he found,
    That bolting would not do it,
He, brother like, did quite his ground,
    And ne'er came back unto it.
          Vow, &c.

---

* Altered in MS. to " German."

† Brother to Charles, 5th Earl of Moray. Upon his brother's death, 7th October, 1735, he became the 6th Earl. He died in the 66th year of his age, on the 11th December, 1739.

10

Brunstane said it was not fear
   That made him stay behind, man ;
But that he had resolv'd that day
   To sleep in a whole skin, man.
The gout, he said, made him take,
   When battle first began, man ;
But when he heard his Marquis fled,
   He took his heels and ran, man.
           Vow, &c.

11

Sir James of Park, he left his horse
   In the middle of a wall, man ;
And durst not stay to take him out,
   For fear a knight should fall, man ;
And Maien he let such a crack,
   And shewed a pantick fear, man ;
And Craigieheads swore he was shot,
   And curs'd the chance of wear, man.
           Vow, &c.

12

When they march'd on the Sheriff Moor,
   With courage stout and keen, man ;

Who would have thought the Gordons gay,
    That day should quite the green, man.
Auchleacher and Auchanachie,
    And all the Gordon tribe, man ;
Like their great Marquis, they could not
    The smell of powder bide, man.
                    Vow, &c.

13

Glenbuicket cryed, plague on you all,
    For Gordons do no good, man ;
For all that fled this day, it is
    Them of the Seaton blood, man.
Clashtirim said it was not so,
    And that he'd make appear, man ;
For he a Seaton stood that day,
    When Gordons ran for fear, man.
                    Vow, &c.

14

The Gordons they are kittle flaws,
    They'll fight with heart and hand, man ;
When they met in Strathbogie raws
    On Thursday afternoon, man ;

But when the Grants came doun the brae,
   Their Enzie shook for fear, man ;
And all the lairds rode up themselves,
   With horse and riding gear, man.
              Vow, &c.

15

Cluny * plays his game of chess,
   As sure as any thing, man ;
And like the royal Gordons race,
   Gave check unto the King, man.
Without a Queen, its clearly seen,
   This game cannot recover ;
I'd do my best, then in great haste
   Play up the rook Hanover.
          Vow as the Marquis ran,
          Coming from Dumblain, man ;
          Strabogie did beshit itself,
          And Enzie was not clean, man.
              Vow, &c.

* This seems rather Gordon of Cluny than Cluny Macpherson.
The estate of Cluny has passed from the ancient race, though still
possessed by a Gordon.

XII.

The Cheat Detected; or a Hint to Poets.

To the TUNE of KING JOHN and the ABBOT of CANTERBURY.

" By Miss Anne Keith, daughter (youngest) of Mr. Keith, late Envoy at Russia, on the stupid ingratitude of Edinburgh to Colonel Graham, who gave the finest and most magnificent ball ever known in Scotland, and got no notice taken of it." MS. note on a copy of the original broadside, formerly in the possession of the late William Boswell, Esquire, Sheriff of Berwickshire.

These verses are from the pen of the lady who is so admirably delineated under the name of Mrs. Bethune Baliol, by Sir Walter Scott, in the introduction to the Chronicles of the Canongate. She was born in 1736, and died in April 1818. Her death is noticed by Sir Walter, in a letter dated 18th April of that year, addressed to Terry,—"You will be sorry to hear that we have lost our old friend, Mrs. Murray Keith. She enjoyed all her spirits and excellent faculties till within two days of her death, when she was seized with a feverish complaint, which eighty-two years were not calculated to resist. Much tradition, and of the very best kind, has died with this excellent old lady; one of the few persons whose spirits and cleanliness, and freshness of mind and body, made old age lovely and desirable."

Mr. Sharpe, in a note on the song " Oscar's Ghost," No. 70 of Johnson's Scotish Musical Museum, mentions that Miss Keith resided many years in Edinburgh, 51, George Street, keeping house with her elder sister, Miss Jenny, and that Sir Walter Scott told him the lady amused herself in her later years by translating Macpherson's Ossian into verse. What became of the MS, after her decease is not known.

These two ladies were daughters of Robert Keith of Murrayshall, in the county of Peebles. One of their brothers was Sir Robert Murray Keith, the Ambassador, and another, Sir Basil Keith, died Governor of Jamaica. It is understood that the papers and manuscripts of the former gentleman are in the possession of the Earl of Hardwicke. Various particulars relative to the family occur in Lord Lyndsay's delightful Lives of the Lindsays. Vol. ii. p. 188.

1

I'LL tell you a story, pray gentles draw. near,
Of Græme and his balls for the future beware;
He has played you a trick that you little suspected,
But rog'ry, like murder, is always detected.
    Derry down, down, &c.

2

On the eighteenth what zeal in your faces was seen,
When summoned by him to drink health to the Queen;
You thought what he did was with upright design,
And all that you drank was the juice of the vine.
    Derry down, &c.

3

Holyrood was illumined, enlivened each guest :
How brilliant the ball ! how superb was the Feast !
How splendid the gall'ry when all went to sup ;
Ah ! who could have dreaded a snake in the cup.

   Derry down, &c.

4

The Beaux were so witty, the Belles looked so bright,
And Græme and his Kitty so kind and polite ;
The Loves and the Graces so blended the whole,
That pleasure there reigned without check or controul.

   Derry down, &c.

5

Who the deuce could have dreamt that from Lethe
  imported,
Some hogsheads by Hermes were slily transported ;
The rogue of a Græme brib'd the rogue of a God,
To convert all the wine with a touch of his rod.

   Derry down, &c.

6

When the whispering and ogling, and toasting and laughing,
Little thought the poor guests what a dose they were
  quaffing ;

But alas! the effects may the dullest convince,
Oblivion and silence have reigned ever since.
    Derry down, &c.

7

Prose writers were render'd unfit to tell facts,
Even truth was silenced by repeated attacks ;
Each poet and poetess had a deep dose,
There was gratitude lulled to a thorough repose.
    Derry down, &c.

8

How long, cry'd the Græme, will the charm have effect,
Pray Heaven ! thàt no spy may the rog'ry detect ;
Friend Hermes, I've lost all the aim of my plot,
If me and my Ball are not henceforth forgot.
    Derry down, &c.

9

For a fortnight 'twill last, on the word of a God,
Or I'll forfeit, says Hermes, my cap and my rod ;
A wonder, you know, can but hold out nine days,
And I'll give you five more to secure you from praise.
    Derry down, &c.

10

Awake and revenge it ye dealers in rhyme,
Tho' late, let him rue such an unheard of crime ;
Let poems on poems be heaped up like Babel,
And poets like harpers encircle his table.

      Derry down, &c.

11

May the wife of his bosom in rhyme still address him,
And his daughter beloved, with verses oppress him ;
May the Muses and Phœbus unite to perplex him,
And grant me a patent poetick to vex him.

      Derry down, &c.

XIII.

The Windy Writer.

These verses, used to be sung by a lady who died twenty years
since at an advanced age. She mentioned they were popular
when she was young, but could give no explanation as to the
parties referred to. Her maiden name was Cunninghame,
and she married a Writer to the Signet of the name of Imlach,
whom she survived.

1

There lives a lass just at the Cross,
   Her face is like the paper,
And she's forsaken Lairds and Lords
   And ta'en a windy writer.

2

And he can neither write nor 'dite,
   And is it not great folly,
We'll send him to the school again,
   Sing cut and dry, Dolly.

3

Cut and dry's for gentleman,
　And corn and hay for horses,
Salt and sugar for auld wives,
　And bonny lads for lasses.

4

And when he comes back fra' the school,
　'Tis hoped he'll be much brighter;
So here's success to the bonny lass,
　And her spouse the windy writer.

XIV.

Pleasures of a Country Life.

From a MS. formerly belonging to James Anderson, the Antiquarian, and now in the Library of the Faculty of Advocates.

1

You nymphs that will true pleasure learn,
There is no comfort in a churn,
The milk-maid sits beneath the cow,
While sheep doth bleat and oxen low;
And if this is the pleasure of being a wife,
Fate defend me from a country life.

2

The team comes in, the ploughboy whistles,
The great dog barks, the turkey-cock bristles,
The ravens they croak, the magpie doth chatter,
And the ducks they cry Quack, quack, in the water;
And if this is the pleasure of being a wife,
Fate defend me from a country life.

3

To live upon butter, with curds and whey,
Deliver me, I heartily pray,
Lean beef and fat pork, for to mend the matter,
Brought in a slovenly great wooden platter;
And if this is the pleasure of being a wife,
Fate defend me from a country life.

4

The hogs they grunt for wash and swill,
In comes the dairy-maid, and calls for Will
To give them some meat to keep them from bawling;
The geese and the peacocks make such a squalling;
And if this is the pleasure of being a wife,
Fate defend me from a country life.

XV.

The Cardinal's Coach Couped.

The second title of this Ballad, as given in the broadside preserved in the Library of the Faculty of Advocates, is—"The
Whigs' Lamentation for the Episcopal Toleration." It
bears to have been printed at London " by John Morphew,
MDCCXI. Price 1d."

1

Alas ! our Kirk has gat a scoup
Upon her covenanted doup,
I fear she run the gantland loup,
   For all the Leagues,
The Cardinal has got a coup,
    With's *Dutch* intrigues.

2

For fear Sacheverel should worrie
Our darling Kirk, he in a hurrie
Gets up, and cries Poor Folk of Currie
   Again we'll be,
Unless you Sighing Sisters stir ye,
    And join with me.
Y

3

He made more haste than was good speed,
Poor man, he couped arse o're head,
For which our hearts were like to bleed,
      When we it saw,
His very coach-horse out of dread,
        Him would not draw.

4

Such overturning is not common,
I fear it prove a fatal omen,
And rouse the courage of the *Roman*
      And curate loons,
To Bothuel Bridge then we shall go, man,
      Get they their gowns.

5

Alas! our sport is like to spill,
Since we have lost our Billie *Will*,
A man may see of little skill
      We'l be undone,
Get they a Toleration Bill,
      We'l change our tune.

6

And truely I think it's no wonder,
Tho' we meet with a clap of thunder;
Considering how great a blunder,
   Of no old date
Say what we will, we labour under,
    In Kirk and State.

7

For now the Government well sees,
We preach the things we don't practise;
The gilded bait that dims our eyes
    Is pride and self,
Tho' vanity we do idolize,
    Yet more our self.

8

Again it's known that Presbytry
Can ne'er consist with monarchy;
Our kingdom, crown, antiquity,
    At last we sold,
A thing will make our memory
    Stink when it's told.

9

Murder of kings or abdication,
Are most conspicuous demonstration
Of Presbyterian moderation.
                    We only want
To take the oath of abjuration
                    To make a Saint.

10

But now I see the Government,
With this Prelatick Parliament,
To cast us off are fully bent ;
                    So let us be
Upon our guard the more intent
                    Before we flee.

11

Saul in a strait to Witch of Endor,
And Sweden's king to Turk at Bender
Made their address ; so let us render
                    What e're befall,
Our kirk and cause to one that's tender
                    Of our caball.

12

Then my advice if you will hear,
The fittest man is Major Weir;
Let's yelp and yell till he appear
    With's staff in hand.
I think we need the less to fear
    If he command.

13

He'll leave the gloomy shades below,
Some stratagem to us he'll show,
How we may reach a fatal blow
    To Prelacie;
Or of our danger let us know
    The certaintie.

14

With rousty rappiers in our hands,
Spades, forks, and graips, as we demand,
Like Egypt's locusts, thro' the land
    We'll fill each place;
And march in covenanted band,
    Like babes of grace.

15

And if we chance to lose the field,
Forc'd to the curat lowns to yield;
We'l take our heels for the best shield,
                And from some sister,
Beneath her petticoat get bield,
                In our great mister.

16

And yet I cannot shun to smile,
When I think on the canting stile
We used in our late exile,
                To mend our breeks;
For well I mind it all the while,
                We grew like Greeks.

17

For our extemporary lecture,
We drank the purest of the nectar,
When once my lady's woman deckt her;
                And which was best,
The laird himself durst not us Hector,
                Tho' her we drest.

18

You need not think I'm speaking lies,
Bear witness house of Cherry-trees,
Where Dainty Davy * strove to please
　　　　My lady's daughter;
And boldly crept beneath her thighs,
　　　　For fear of slaughter.

---

* The celebrated David Williamson, minister of the West Kirk,
who, when pursued by General Dalyell's troopers, was hid by the
Lady Cherry-trees in her daughter's bed, and availed himself of that
opportunity to add to the population. Cherry-trees is near Kelso,
and belonged to a family of the name of Murray. His exploit on
that memorable occasion was celebrated in a song called Dainty Davy,
adapted to an old air of the same name, still popular, and which appears in Playford's Dancing Master, 1657. See Whitelaw's Book of
Scottish Song, Glasgow 1843, p. 98.

XVI.

Tom Linn.

(A Fragment.)

The following fragment of the interesting ballad of Tom Linn
or Tamlane was taken down from the recitation of an old
woman—it contains numerous deviations from the copy
printed in the Border Minstrelsy, (Scott's Poetical Works,
Vol. ii, p. 337,) and on that account has been included in
this little volume.

1

O ! all you ladies young and gay,
　　Who are so sweet and fair ;
Do not go into Chaster's wood,
　　For Tomlin will be there.

*　　*　　*　　*　　*　　*　　*

2

Fair Margaret sat in her bonny bower,
　　Sewing her silken seam ;
And wished to be in Chaster's wood,
　　Among the leaves so green.

3

She let the seam fall to her foot,
    The needle to her toe;
And she has gone to Chaster's wood,
    As fast as she could go.

4

When she began to pull the flowers,
    She pull'd both red and green;
Then by did come, and by did go,
    Said, " Fair maid let abene.

5

" O ! why pluck you the flowers, lady,
    " Or why climb you the tree;
" Or why come ye to Chaster's wood
    " Without the leave of me ?"

6

" O ! I will pull the flowers," she said,
    " Or I will break the tree,
" For Chaster's wood it is my own;
    " I'll ask no leave at thee."

7

He took her by the milk-white hand,
    And by the grass-green sleeve ;
And laid her down upon the flowers,
    At her he ask'd no leave.]

8

The lady blush'd and sourly frown'd,
    And she did think great shame ;
Says, " If you are a gentleman,
    " You will tell me your name."

9

" First they did call me Jack," he said,
    " And then they call'd me John ;
" But since I liv'd in the fairy court,
    " Tomlin has always been my name.

10

" So do not pluck that flower, lady,
    " That has these pimples gray ;
" They would destroy the bonny babe
    " That we've gotten in our play,"

11

" O ! tell to me, Tomlin," she said,
" And tell it to me soon ;
" Was you ever at a good church door,
" Or got you Christendom ?"

12

" O ! I have been at good church door,
" And oft her yetts within ;
" I was the laird of Foulis's son,
" The heir of all his land.

13

" But it fell once upon a day,
" As hunting I did ride ;
" As I rode east and west yon hill,
" There woe did me betide.

14

" O ! drowsy, drowsy as I was,
" Dead sleep upon me fell ;
" The Queen of fairies she was there,
" And took me to hersel.

15

" The morn at even is Hallowe'en,
  " Our fairy court will ride
" Through England and Scotland both,
  " Through all the world wide;
" And if that ye would me borrow,
  " At Rides Cross ye may bide.

16

" You may go into the Miles Moss,
  " Between twelve hours and one;
" Take holy water in your hand,
  " And cast a compass round.

17

" The first court that comes along,
  " You'll let them all pass by;
" The next court that comes along,
  " Salute them reverently.

18

" The next court that comes along,
  " Is clad in robes of green ;
" And it's the head court of them all,
  " For in it rides the Queen.

19

" And I upon a milk-white steed,
   " With a gold star in my crown ;
" Because I am an earthly man,
   " I'm next the Queen in renown.

20

" Then seize upon me with a spring,
   " Then to the ground I'll fa' ;
" And then you'll hear a rueful cry,
   " That Tomlin is awa'.

21

" Then I'll grow in your arms two,
   " Like to a savage wild ;
" But hold me fast, let me not go,
   " I'm father of your child.

22

" I'll grow into your arms two
   " Like an adder, or a snake ;
" But hold me fast, let me not go,
   " I'll be your earthly maik.

23

" I'll grow into your arms two,
  " Like ice on frozen lake ;
" But hold me fast, let me not go,
  " Or from your goupen break.

24

" I'll grow into your arms two,
  " Like iron in strong fire ;
" But hold me fast, let me not go,
  " Then you'll have your desire."

25

And its next night into Miles Moss,
  Fair Margaret has gone ;
When lo she stands beside Rides Cross,
  Between twelve hours and one.

26

There's holy water in her hand,
  She casts a compass round ;
And presently a fairy band
  Comes riding o'er the mound.

*   *   *   *   *   *   *

XVII.

The Lady's Complaint.

ritten by Lord Binning, as to whom, see Walpole's Royal
and Noble Authors.—PARK'S EDITION.

1

A LADY made a great complaint,
　　A little while ago;
She seemed to be in great despair
　　About a cook or two.

2

But what's a nasty creeshy cook,
　　To fill a heart with woe?
When folks complain they never think
　　What others undergo.

3

These many years I've rid about,
　　And never had a skirt;
So you may guess my petticoats
　　Have aye been in the dirt.

4

And dirt's a thing I cannot thole,
   Yet dirt I must go thro';
I kenna how to get a skirt,
   Or what to mak it o'.

5

I fain wad wear a camblet skirt,
   My petticoats aboon ;
But camblet's an untasty thing,
   And it would wear out soon,

6

If I should make a washing thing,
   It soon would flimsy be ;
And all the laughing loons would make
   A laughing stock of me.

7

For any one who's making wabs,
   It would be little work ;
To add some five or six plies
   Of good Turk upon Turk.

8

'Twould last me a my days, I'm sure,
  And would look very douse;
But then, I fear, I'd be a lump,
  And look as big's a house.

9

I cannot make it to my mind,
  To want it is a load;
In short I must not ride at all,
  And there's the upshot o'd.

XVIII.

The Downfall of Cockburn's Meeting House.

To the TUNE of COME SIT THEE DOWN MY PHILLIS.

The following song of triumph upon the destruction of the
Episcopal chapel of the Rev. Mr. Cockburn in Glasgow has
been carefully preserved by Wodrow, and is now in the
Library of the Faculty of Advocates. It is a most delightful specimen of the Presbyterian muse, and is worthy of the
important national event it was intended to commemorate.
" Curate " Cockburn, as he was designated by his opponents,
was a bitter thorn in the side of poor Wodrow,—he was
zealous, able, and popular, and had occasioned much annoy-
ance by his denying the validity of Presbyterian baptism,—
hence the destruction of his chapel, or meeting-house, as it was
then contemptuously called, was a laudable act in the eyes of
the rigidly righteous. This striking illustration of puritanical
zeal occurred in August 1714. See the Wodrow Correspon-
dence, vol. i. p. 562.

1

WE have not yet forgot, Sir,
    How Cockburn's kirk was broke, Sir ;
The pulpit gown was pulled down,
    And turned into nought, Sir.

2

The pulpit cloth was rent, Sir,
Unto the Cross was sent, Sir;
The boys that did convoy it
Were into prison put, Sir.

3

The Chess-windows they were broke, Sir,
Out o're the window cast, Sir;
With a convoy of holo hoi,
Unto the streets were sent, Sir.

4

The French are disappointed,
Their wicked plots disjointed;
Poor Cockburn he's affronted,
But the Whiggs they're advanced.

5

Long necked Peggie H[ome], Sir,
Did weep and stay at home, Sir;
'Cause poor Cockburn and his wife
Were forc'd to flee the town, Sir.

6

And after they were gone, Sir,
They went to Stirling town, Sir ;
They thought with their heart and mind
To get poor Jamie home, Sir.

7

But they were disappointed,
And their wicked plots disjointed ;
We'll make them all run and cry,
Oh ! we're disappointed.

8

Their Highland King for fear, Sir,
Was put in such a steer, Sir ;
We made his breeks have such stink,
That none could him come near, Sir.

9

Macdonald is his name, Sir,
Of him you may think shame, Sir ;
A Highlander whose name stinks,
You Popish rogue go home, Sir.

10

The Chess-window did reel, Sir,
Like to a spinning wheel, Sir ;
For Dagon he is fall'n now,
I hope he'll never rise, Sir.

11

Some say thir lines were compos'd
By boys in grammar school, Sir ;
What they've said, they are ador'd ;
Amen, so let it be, Sir.

XIX.

Glasgow's Parrad.

To the TUNE of THE WINTER IS COLD, MY CLEEDING IS THIN.

The Original, now in the Library of the Faculty of Advocates,
   formerly belonged to Wodrow. From its minute description
   of the proceedings at Glasgow, on occasion of the Corona-
   tion of George I., it has been inserted in this little Collection.

COME all ye Protestants give ear to my song,
The *Jacobite*-party they thought to do wrong,
To have a *Pretender* our King for to be,
But they're prevented, we bless the Most Hie.

Queen *Ann* is departed and *Harlay's* brought down ;
King *George* is anointed and mounted the throne,
The *Whiggs* are advanced our heads for to be,
Much joy is expressed among the clergie.

The churches did meet, and thought on the same,
Appointed a day to thank and proclaim,
God's works to declare that wonderfull be,
Ascribing the praises unto the Most Hie.

That he so appeared King *George* to advance,
In spite of *Pretender*, the *Pope*, and of *France*,
And all their complyers tho' they be hie,
He'll give them defyance whatever they be.

The day is appointed his crown to set on,
These news are proclaimed in city and town,
All things are provided that necessar be,
For advancing the honour of his clemencie.

What might be their labour iuto other towns,
We cannot declare it, but in our own bounds ;
And *Glasgow* the chiefest in every degree,
They may well declare the same who did see.

October the twenty, when day did begin,
The Magistrates mounted, and nobles came in,
The burgesses meet in every degree,
Appointed their way for solemnitie.

At twelve of the clock their drums they went throw,
Acquainted the people how that they must bow,
And yeeld with submission, what e'er might be,
The hopes that they had of bastard *Jamie*.

At two afternoon they might well be seen,
So properly mounted, approaching the green,
With collors display'd, in wind they did flee,
I dare well declare a pretty Meinzie.

With sword and with gun as clear as the steel,
And cocks on their hats, as set them full well;
With ribban at sword as low as their knee,
With right pretty poses as ever might be;

They planted their ground, so rested a while,
But e're it was long, they're heard off a mile
With oyes most loud, their hats they did flee,
And all was for joy, King *George* was so hie.

Before five o'clock they returned again,
Approached the town a right stately train;
With flourished collors full pleasant to see,
The bells they did ring with sweet melodie.

Frae once they were planted each man at the cross,
There might none go by, on foot or on horse;
They did stand most stately as ever might be,
Their guns they discharged in highest degree.

The Magistrates stood, and their officers still,
And gave them their word what e're was their will;
The same they obeyed in every degree,
Their swords they unsheathed, and hats they did flee.

They sent up some men, and they took off the cock
From off the Tolbooth, wherein stood their knock;
They mounted a lamp as great as might be,
With many great candles, that people might see.

The bon-fires burnt in all parts of the town,
For joy of King *George* they made this renown;
Then lighted their candles so thick as might be,
Although a dark night, you money might see.

To ly on the streets, or to change if ye will,
For wine and good brandy to drink of your fill;
You needed no guides, what ever you be,
To find out a lodging in all that citie.

The bells they did ring, the shots they did roar,
There was ne're a *Scotsman* the like saw before;
Such animose joy in every degree,
And all for King *George* his High Majestie.

I wish our Great Soveraign now on the throne,
Had been in brave *Glasgow* to see what was done,
For honour and joy of his Majestie,
That he was come over our King for to be.

The fires did burn till late in the night,
And candles continued still in our sight;
No darkness nor grief at all we did see,
But each one rejoicing in every degree.

The gallants they travelled still up and down,
And still the brave bon-fires compassed round:
They drank the good-wine in the highest degree,
And then the brave glasses they mounted full hie.

There was to be seen as ye passed along,
In many glass-windows the rest was among;
In legible letters that any might see,
God save our King *George* in peace and safetie.

Some for their great honour the rest was above,
Whereby for their profit I hope it shall prove;
Did keep a free table with so great plentie,
Where all was made welcome, what ever they be.

I pray you, brave Magistrats, pardon me all,
And also ye officers, both great and small;
That order these men so pleasant to see,
For this my poor scribble to venture so hie.

For tho' I be not a great man of the state,
Nor yet a great lawyer for ending debate;
Yet I let you to know, whatever you be,
I pray for his Majesty as well as ye.

XX.

Bold Rankin.

The following is from a MS. copy in the possession of W. H. Logan, Esquire, derived from oral tradition. It is exceedingly curious, as being quite a new version of the old Ballad called "Lammikin," for which see Finlay's Ballads, Vol. ii. pp. 47 and 57, as also Herd's Scots Songs, Vol. i. p. 145. Whether the present is the original Ballad must of course remain a matter of doubt; but it has this advantage at least, that the appellation bestowed upon the hero is more intelligible than that of the mysterious "Lammikin."

SAID the Lord to his Lady,
  Beware of Rankin;
For I am going to England
  To wait on the King.

No fears, no fears,
  Said the Lady, said she;
For the doors shall be bolted
  And the windows pindee.

Go bar all the windows,
  Both outside and in;
Don't leave a window open
  To let bold Rankin in.

She has barred all the windows,
  Both outside and in ;
But she left one of them open
  To let bold Rankin in.

O where is the master of this house,
  Said bold Rankin ?
He's up in Old England,
  Said the false nurse to him.

O where is the mistress of this house,
  Said bold Rankin ?
She's up in the chamber sleeping,
  Said the false nurse to him.

O how shall we get her down,
  Said bold Rankin ?
By piercing the baby,
  Said the false nurse to him.

Go please the baby, nursy O,
  Go please it with a bell ;
It will not be pleased, madam,
  Till you come down yoursel.

How can I come down stairs
  So late into the night,
Without coal or candle
  To shew me the light ?

There is a silver bolt lies
   On the chest head;
Give it to the baby,—
   Gave it sweet milk and bread.

She rammed the silver bolt
   Up the baby's nose;
Till the blood it came trinkling down
   The baby's fine clothes.

Go please the baby, nursy,
   Go please it with the bell;
It will not please, madam,
   Till you come down yoursel.

It will neither please with breast milk,
   Nor yet with pap;
But I pray, loving Lady,
   Come and roll it in your lap.

The first step she stepit,
   She steppit on a stone;
And the next step she stepit
   She met bold Rankin.

O Rankin, O Rankin,
   Spare me till twelve o'clock,
And I will give you as many guineas
   As you can carry on your back.

What care I for as many guineas
    As seeds into a sack;
When I cannot keep my hands
    Off your lily white neck?

O will I kill her, nursy,
    Or let her abee?
O kill her said the false nurse,
    She was never good to me.

Go scour the bason, Lady,
    Both outside and in;
To hold your mother's heart's blood,
    Sprung from a noble kin.

To hold my mother's heart's blood
    Would make my heart full woe,
O rather kill me, Rankin,
    And let my mother go.

Go scour the bason, servants,
    Both outside and in,
To hold your Lady's heart's blood,
    Sprung from a noble kin.

To hold my Lady's heart's blood
    Would make my heart full woe;
O rather kill me, Rankin,
    And let my Lady go.

Go scour the bason, nursy,
   Both outside and in,
To hold your Lady's heart's blood,
   Sprung from a noble kin.

To hold my Lady's heart's blood
   Would make my heart full glad;
Ram in the knife bold Rankin,
   And gar the blood to shed.

She's none of my comrades,
   She's none of my kin;
Ram in the knife, bold Rankin,
   And gar the blood rin.

O will I kill her, nursy,
   Or let her abee?
O kill her, said the false nurse,
   She was never good to me.

   *   *   *   *

" I wish my wife and family
   May be all well at home ;
For the silver buttons of my coat
   They will not stay on."

As Betsy was looking
   O'er her window so high,
She saw her dear father
   Come riding by.

" O father, dear father,
    Don't put the blame on me;
It was false nurse and Rankin
    That killed your Lady."

O was'nt that an awful sight,
    When he came to the stair;
To see his fairest Lady
    Lie bleeding there?

The false nurse was burnt
    On the mountain hill head;
And Rankin was boiled
    In a pot full of lead.

Finis.

EDINBURGH: LAURIE AND CO.